Matthew Yancey

Taking the High Road Series #2

Morris Fenris

Matthew Yancey, Taking the High Road Series #2

Table of Contents

Chapter 1

"Star! Hey, Star! You're lookin' mighty pretty today."

Franklin Bower again. Somehow he had found her, even though she had moved from her favorite marketplace down near the wharf, just because of his unwanted advances. Ignoring the importunate call, she continued unloading items from her small wagon to arrange onto the plank table set up.

Soft, well-tanned pelts taken from beaver and wolf, fur pieces, bowls and vases made of fired clay, jewelry put together with silver wire and colorful glass beads, deerskin moccasins, leather hand-tooled belts, shining solid silver buckles: all laid out to attract the most attention from passersby.

Except for Franklin Bower.

He had discovered her shift in whereabouts from the height of his palomino stallion, and was now riding slowly around and around the new field of operation to fully inspect what was going on. "You got some fresh stuff on your cart today, girl? Well, now, ain't seen them bolo ties before. Looks like blue agate, outa the hills. Holy crow, Star, your maw'll try puttin' together just about anything to sell, won't she?"

No response. Still mounted, leaning forward with one arm resting on the saddle horn, Bower kept on leisurely circling, like the swoop of a hawk overhead in search of prey.

"Does that include you, Goldenstar Mendoza?" he asked in a low, insinuating voice.

That reached her. Despite the heat, chills raced up her spine and back down again, but cold fire darkened her pretty amber eyes to smoke. "It does not. I have refused your offers since you first started making them, Mr. Bower. What makes you think I would now change my mind?"

He grinned. A brash, bulky man, his thick black hair curled with sweat under a wide-brimmed hat, his mustache badly in need of a trim, he oozed something that might, in some circles, be considered charm. Flinging one leg over his horse's rump, he climbed down, hitched the reins to a post, and stepped up onto the wooden walkway.

"Oh, Star, you know I'll keep on a-tryin'. You got your stuff laid out in such nice order, I think I'll just have to inspect your wares."

The young woman had set up her outdoor shop outside the Hotel Alexandria. Across the narrow dusty street, two men idled on a bench in front of the Hanrahan Saloon. One in particular, Sheriff William Goddard, was keeping an interested eye on these proceedings that might require intervention.

"Somethin' goin' on over there?" his companion asked, curious.

"Could be. Bower's a rancher, comes into town now and then, and trouble somehow seems to follow him wherever he goes."

"Looks like he's bein' a nuisance to that Indian girl. Then it's okay in San Francisco to sell goods on a street corner like that?"

Goddard stretched his legs out and crossed one ankle over the other. "Ain't no ord'nance against it. 'Course, the city council may get it into their heads to make some damn fool changes." He glanced sideways. "I take it that sorta thing can't be allowed in Charleston?"

"Not that I know of. Nor in Santone." Matthew Yancey took another cautious sip of the piss-poor brew that passed for coffee and slowly shook his head of rather shaggy black hair. "Will, did you ever consider gettin' someone else to make the pot of joe every mornin', 'stead of doin' it yourself?"

"First order of the day, son. Whatsamatter, you don't like the taste?"

Matt grinned. "Oh, it's fine, just fine. Puts lead in your pencil, if nothin' else. Just thinkin' of savin' you some time, that's all."

"Hmmph." The sort of half-snort that worked well for male communication when there was nothing more to be said. "Didn't have t'pay for it, didja?"

"Oh, I b'lieve I will be doin' just that, in more ways than one."

From under level brows, Goddard thoughtfully studied his new friend. "Yeah, you may be right. Nice of you to stay on here for a while, after your brother's weddin', only b'cause I asked you to."

Matt was gazing out over the street scene, with pedestrian traffic, horse traffic, and wagon traffic stirring up noise and dust, seemingly oblivious—just enjoying the usual fine weather of San Francisco, thank you very much—yet acutely aware of every detail. Especially the scene being played out between rancher and Indian girl: cajolery and ribald comments from one; from the other, frozen chunks of a response bitten off here and there between hard white teeth.

"Lot of bad stuff goin' in the world right now," he said soberly.

"You got that straight. Part of the reason I'm glad you're here, Matt. Didn't know if the Rangers could spare you though."

Another sip of the godawful coffee, almost cold now, which made it even less palatable. "Reckon my captain figured, since I'd already come this far north and west to get young John married off, I may as well have a little more time to myself, lookin' around. He gave me permission to extend my leave, anyway."

"Mighty white of him. Tell me again how you happened to join up?"

For a brief moment, Matt was lost in time, harking back to events over the past few years, and beyond. His boyhood on the sprawling cotton plantation outside Charleston. His wedding to Elisa Nolan, daughter of a neighboring planter. The birth of baby Robert Yancey, some twelve months later, and the death of his beloved wife from childbed fever.

Malachai Yancey, patriarch and owner of Belle Clare, took sick the next year. He lingered long enough to give over advice for each of his ten sons and was subsequently buried in the family plot, next to the boys' mother, Clarissa, gone to heaven this quarter of a century ago.

The Belle Clare heirs had discussed the current volatile political situation, and what Matthew had conjectured was the handwriting on the wall: some sort of eventual, crucial clash between north and south, with every denizen caught in the middle. A joint, unanimous decision had led the Yanceys to sell their plantation, and each had eventually struck out on their own.

For Matthew, this meant leaving behind whatever troubles might be brewing in his home state and taking his motherless son and a nursemaid/governess, the widowed Sarah Coleman, to Texas. There, settling in, he had applied for and been accepted as a member of the Rangers, helping to defend the Texas frontier.

Under the leadership of Captain John Salmon "Rip" Ford, in 1858 an expeditionary force, made up of Matt and some hundred others, set out to attack the Comanche, after their series of raids on homesteading settlers in the Red River area. With that battle successfully concluded, the following year saw Ford's Rangers engaged in another action against and defeat of a local Mexican rancher, Juan Cortina, who had been harassing local landowners around Brownsville.

Matt had seen plenty of conflict during the last few years. He wanted to see no more. He longed for peace, and security, and a quiet place to raise his son. The news of yet another war, this one arisen between factions of his country, was disheartening.

At least he could feel that his judgment had been vindicated, and his decision to leave for a new land the right one, when South Carolina seceded from the Union in December, just last year. Then came the secession of Texas on February 1, the formation of Confederate states on February 9, and the firing on Fort Sumter in April, a mere four months ago.

He had no taste for more strife, more battles, more blood. Having left all that behind, he could only hope that what was going on back east would not ripple westward as far as California, to engulf more victims.

In answer to Goddard's question, he gave a brief history of his more recent adventures, ending with the fact that his plans for the future lay somewhat in limbo.

"It's a nasty business, what's goin' on with our citizens across the nation," said the sheriff quietly, after a few minutes. "I'd like to think we're well out of it."

"So you're expectin' trouble?"

"Not necessarily. But sometimes you get some trigger-happy yahoos from both sides of the fence in any fight, determined to cause trouble, and all hell can break loose."

"Sorta like what's goin' on over there, across the street?" The slight tilt of Matt's head indicated the encounter between potential customer and proprietor at her marketplace stand. No violence, no real harassment yet; just, for the moment, mild annoyance, as indicated by a cool fix of facial expression and a non-response to any comment. "What's her story again?"

Shifting position, leaning a little forward to rest both elbows across his wool-clad thighs, the sheriff surveyed his territory. "Ah, Goldenstar, you mean. Her folks live up in the hills, but she's got herself a nice little cabin at the edge of town."

"What's that stuff she's put out for sale?"

"Her paw is a Mexican trapper," Goddard explained, "Daniel Mendoza, married to Star's mama, a Cherokee woman named Adsila. Pretty woman. Easy to see where the girl comes by her looks. But the folks keep mostly to themselves, ever since that massacre, up by Eureka."

A slight frown of heavy black brows recalling the faulty memory. "I heard some about that, but not the details."

"Helluva thing. It happened about a year and a half ago, when a bunch of crazy white militia people attacked the Wiyot tribe, on

8

Indian Island. It was a slaughter, Matt. Babies, kids, women, old men…blood and dead bodies everywhere. Made you sick to your stomach."

"No provocation, if I recall."

"None whatsoever."

The lawman in Matt stirred up to grimace. "And nobody rounded up and hauled off to trial for the cold-blooded murder of more'n a hundred innocent people."

"Not yet, and never likely t'be. So, with some bad feelin's toward Indians roundabout, Star's folks keep to themselves. She comes into the center of town every so often, like this—brings their handmade commodities to sell. Does quite well with it, from what I've seen."

Matt glanced once again at the wagon, the patient mule hitched up in the shade, and the entrepreneur plying her trade. "Seems like she might be takin' quite a chance bein' on her own, if you think somebody might be out to cause problems."

"Ah, not s'much because of her background. More just the low-life scum—like Bower, over there—that doesn't respect any woman. He bothers Star ev'ry time he can, so I keep an eye on him and boot him back to his ranch if it gets too bad." Goddard snorted and shifted position so that the wooden bench creaked a little, in protest. "Damned pain in the ass."

Across the street, new customers had just approached the temporary marketplace. Customers much more welcome than the present one, it was safe to report.

"Good morning, Goldenstar. You're looking well."

At the sound of a female voice, the girl turned with relief from her busy work of rearranging painted clay bowls—work only undertaken to avoid Franklin Bower's continued presence at the outer edges of her booth. "Miss Goddard," she greeted the newcomer with a smile. "How nice to see you again."

"And a good day t'you, too," said Bower from behind the table, tipping his hat. He hated being ignored by anyone. And by the

Sheriff's sister, one of the pillars of the community, no less—it was not to be borne.

Frances Goddard, tall, regal, and supremely self-confident, sent a cool glance sideways. "Mr. Bower," she acknowledged. "In town visiting from the ranch, are you?"

"Yes, ma'am. Had some business t'take care of—layin' claim to more property. Gonna have the biggest spread in all of California, soon," he boasted. "And then I run into Star, here, and stopped to shoot the breeze a little."

"Did you, now?" Frances exchanged a significant look with her companion.

Her companion: another woman of similar age, whose straw hat sat tipped at a becoming angle over gray-streaked hair, pulled back into a neat bun. Though her frame resembled one of Star's squatty clay vases, her kindly faded blue eyes looked out onto the world with interest and compassion, and her hand rested lightly but compellingly on the shoulder of a small dark-haired boy standing beside her. Having no concern with adult conversation, he was craning his neck to look over the display items.

"Forgive me, I must make some introductions," Frances said cheerfully. "Sarah, this is Goldenstar Mendoza, who lives in the area. Along with her parents, she's become a real businesswoman. For a number of years, I had the pleasure of Star's attendance in my schoolroom. And her high marks put several older students to shame, let me tell you. Oh, and Franklin Bower. A rancher, as you heard."

"Ladies." Bower tipped his sombrero again, offering an ingratiating smile. "And you are—?"

"I'm Mrs. Sarah Coleman." She stepped forward immediately, with a firm handshake all around, and a smile. "I'm the housekeeper for Mr. Matthew Yancey, and I also keep watch over his son, young Master Rob, here."

"I'm so pleased to make your acquaintance, Mrs. Coleman. And yours, too, Rob." Star returned the friendly gesture with her own lovely smile that included the whole group. "Have you recently relocated to San Francisco?"

"They traveled up from Texas a month or so ago," Frances interceded, "When Mr. Yancey's brother was married."

Bower, still feeling ignored and out of sorts, shifted from one foot to the other and interjected himself with apparent authority. "Yeah, I saw somethin' about that in the newspaper. Woman from Boston, come here with lotsa cash in her pocket. A good match—her rich, him poor. Money talks."

The disparaging tone was guaranteed to draw Star's attention. Fine brows drawn together, lovely generous mouth set now into ungenerous lines, she sent a scorching look from his boots to the top of his head. "Not if they were happy with each other. In that case, money doesn't matter."

"So, then." He sent the same look in return, from her beaded moccasins to her shining black braids, except that his was coarse rather than contemptuous. "All the fortune I've put together don't impress you one iota?"

A flash of the long-lashed amber eyes, angry only because she had allowed her dislike of the man to provoke her.

Frances, protective as always of her former student, stepped into the fray. "We mustn't keep you from your important business, Mr. Bower," she said firmly. "This is just women's talk, anyway; nothing for you to be interested in."

A dull flush rose into the rancher's unshaven cheeks. Dismissed, just like that: calmly and easily. Damned bitch. "Then I'll say good day to you, ladies." Two fingers touched the brim of his hat in a small salute, and he turned away. Only to toss back what he knew was the last word: "I'll catch up with you later, Star, and we'll have us a little powwow then."

"Nasty heathen," muttered Frances, watching him climb onto his horse and canter away.

"Do you think he takes rather a lot on himself?" Sarah wondered. "My dear, we seem to have happened upon you at an opportune time."

"Deliberately, I'm sure," said Star, with a glance of warm appreciation for her rescuers. "Have you been exploring the town, Miss Goddard?"

"We have, indeed, Star."

It was a fine sun-splashed morning, with plenty of shade provided by shop awnings or an overhanging porch roof, even the incidental scrawny tree. An occasional passerby glanced their way: with chilly detachment, if female; with curiosity and speculation, if male. Several teenaged boys pelted past, their boots thumping on the wooden walkway, their attention shifting sideways to hiss, "Breed! Breed! Half-breed!" as they ran.

To everything, especially the invective, the Cherokee girl seemed oblivious. Defensively so.

"More heathens," muttered Frances disparagingly, and then went on with an explanation: "I met Sarah at Cecelia Powell's wedding, and we struck up a friendship. Since Mr. Yancey appears disposed to linger here indefinitely, she and I have been able to take tea together now and then, and we've twisted my brother's arm to serve as escort for us at the theatre a time or two."

Something quite poignant briefly clouded Star's expression, then as quickly disappeared. "Friendships are important," she agreed quietly. "And have you been shopping, as well?"

"We visited the Emporium," Sarah contributed. "A nice lot of goods there, with plenty of variety. I very much enjoyed seeing some of the latest styles, both in bonnets and dresses." She sighed happily.

"Miss Mendoza."

"Yes, Rob. May I help you?"

"Uh—I was just wonderin'—you got an amount set for those rabbit foot good luck charms?"

For a few minutes the discussion centered on good-natured but determined bartering, on both sides, until Star eventually admitted defeat, to the boy's great delight, and let him name his own price.

It was a congenial group, with the ladies looking like a cluster of spring butterflies in their powder blue muslin and flowery cotton lawn. Summer in San Francisco: lightweight fabric, pastel colors, short sleeves and low necklines. By contrast, Star might have been some exotic bird, flown down from mountain hideaways, in her soft butter-yellow deerskin dress, fringed and feathered and belted by beads.

"Well, you all seem t'be havin' a good time over here," said Sheriff Goddard, approaching. "Matt and me, we reckoned we'd come see what was goin' on."

Frances gave him the sort of withering look only a sister can perfect. "It took you long enough," she sniffed. "Didn't you see that Star was being bothered by that odious Bower person?"

A quick figurative back-pedal, and a vigorous protest: "We were keepin' an eye on the situation. If trouble started, we'd'a been right in the middle of it, jig time. B'sides, Frannie, I knew you'd hold the fellah in line."

"Daddy, look. Daddy, see what I got!" The excited little boy, eager to show off his new purchase, was joggling his father's arm. "The lady—I mean, Miss Mendoza…we worked out a deal, and she gived me a really fair price."

"Did she now?" Smiling, Matt knelt to examine his son's prize with respectful attention. "A rabbit's foot, by golly. You've been wantin' one of those for a long while." Rising to his feet in one lithe movement, his gaze shifted, dark eyes warm with amusement and appreciation. "I take it you're Miss Mendoza," he said, reaching out. "My name is Matthew Yancey, and I thank you for bein' so kind."

She accepted the shake, feeling her fingers being swallowed up by his big firm clasp. And a spark. A definite spark. Maybe even a tingle. Slightly puzzled, she glanced down at their joined hands, then up again at his face. A good-looking, good-humored face, darkened by the day's growth of dark beard, with perceptive dark eyes that surveyed his surroundings with friendliness and favor.

"It was my pleasure," she finally managed to respond without stammering. "Young Rob is well-versed in the ways of bartering, that one."

The man was studying her just as intently. Was it possible that he, too, had felt that small jolt?

"Yes, he's—uh—well, for a five-year-old, Rob is—uh—"

"I've explained that I'm your housekeeper, Mr. Yancey," put in Sarah at this point, with some sensitivity for the tentative first meeting. "Miss Mendoza should know that I've helped with the raising of this fine boy for some time, so I feel I must take credit for the person he's becoming." She finished up with a smile, half-solemn, half-droll, which so brightened her expression that the sheriff, standing nearby, suddenly took notice.

"Say, listen, Frannie, no reason for all of us to stand around jawin' in the street," he commented. "We could get better acquainted at supper tonight, at our house. Think you could put somethin' together by then?"

Frances could never resist a challenge. "I'm sure I can. What about you, young man? Will you be hungry about six o'clock?"

"Sure," agreed Rob, after a quick upward glance at his father for confirmation. "Whatcha havin' for me to eat?"

"For one thing, the chocolate cake I baked and frosted this morning."

The boy's dark eyes, so like his father's, widened. "I like choc'late, Miss Goddard. I really do like choc'late. That'd do me just fine."

The adults laughed, while Matt affectionately ruffled his son's hair.

"And that includes you, too, Star," added Frances, turning toward her. "You know where we live. Will you join us?"

Feeling suddenly shy, she took a small step backward. "Thank you. I'd like that."

"Good, it's all settled then," was the brisk response. "Even if my brother does issue his invitations like a buffalo in a china shop…" Riding roughshod over his blustered protest of "Oh, now, Frannie, no such thing—"

Chapter 2

From his vantage point of a window looking out of Hanrahan's saloon, Franklin Bower watched the group across the street. Convivial conversation, light laughter, interaction with the kid—a pushy little tadpole if Bower had ever seen one—and then eventual dispersion. Frances and Sarah wandered off with their charge in tow. Yancey and the sheriff sauntered away in the direction of his office. And that eyeful and a half, Miss Goldenstar Mendoza, was finally left alone with her stall of goods and a trickle of customers.

Franklin nursed a shot glass of whiskey while he debated the merits of seeking her out again. He wanted her. God damn, he wanted her, this toothsome wench with all her curvy parts in all the right places in all the right order. He wanted her for daytime and he wanted her for bed sport.

Not for anything as meaningful as marriage, of course.

As a half-breed, Star's mixture of Mexican and Indian blood might all come together into one perfect desirable package: the lush black hair that, when unbound, he'd be willing to bet, fell past her waist; the skin like warm Chinese tea, with a little bit of bronze tipped into it; the eyes clear but as changeable as a nugget of amber. And the mouth, blessed with mobility and charm—holy saints above, he could imagine doing great things with and to that mouth.

But all that physical beauty in one perfect desirable package didn't mean she could ever be considered respectable. No, no marriage. Something much less than.

So far he'd been patient. He'd done his best with engaging her, teasing her, wooing her, only to be figuratively slapped down and shunted aside. As if she stood on some high pedestal, far above him, able to look down on all his efforts with contempt!

No, soon all that would be past. He intended to take action and seize what he saw as his, by fair means or foul, come hell or high water. Her friendship with the two Goddards counted for nothing in his opinion; nor did her status with anyone else in this town, which stood on shaky ground.

"Hey, Bower, you randy old son-of-a-bitch, ain't seen much of you lately."

The boisterous voice reached him through a fog of reverie, and he turned his head. "Sykes," he acknowledged the newcomer. "C'mon and sit down."

Beer bottle in one hand, Russell Sykes pulled out a chair to straddle and plunked himself in place. "Been keepin' busy out at the Condor?"

"Fair t' middlin', Russ. And you? What're you up to these days?"

"Ah, just been considerin' some options." With the glugging down of several giant swallows, his Adam's apple bounced around like a rubber ball. "Thought maybe I'd head back east and join up."

Bower looked his surprise. "The hell you say! Why wouldja do such a damn fool thing?"

Silence for a minute. Sykes, pondering the question, rolled the glass bottle back and forth between his palms as if to think through his answer. "I was born and raised in Virginia, Frank. Most of my family still lives there. There's been a mess of fightin' roundabout, and I'd like t' get in on it, do what I can. Seems only right, y' know."

"One of our valiant boys in gray, then."

At the faint hint of sarcasm in that tone, Sykes shot a suspicious glance toward his companion. "Y'think I'm only interested in wearin' some fancy uniform?"

"No, Russ. Not a bit of it. Just wonderin'—you seem to have a pretty good life here. Why go outa your way to risk takin' a bullet? You wanna be a martyr, dyin' for the cause?"

"A good life?" Brushing back a forelock of tumbled red hair, Sykes stared at his companion. "If you mean sunshine and wide open spaces, you'd be right on that score. But I'm off and on between jobs, no trainin' for anything in particular, no steady income. Without money, Frank, a good life ain't so very good."

Tapping his shot glass softly and reflectively on the table top, Bower returned his gaze to the window and his prey across the street. With the blend of two cultures— one passionate and demonstrative, the other more stoic, constrained—Goldenstar Mendoza presented a challenge. And a promise.

"Well, don't go ridin' off into the sunset just yet," he advised. "I might have a job for you to do in the near future."

Chapter 3

If not for the loyalty of her male customers, Star reflected soberly, this business, she did her best to manage, would hardly be viable at all, since the virtuous ladies of this town would have little to do with her on the best of days. It was probably just as well they weren't aware—or chose not to ask—as to where their husbands had picked up those lovely agate earrings, or the hand-loomed rug for their entryway, or the tooled leather saddlebag thrown so casually over a horse's rump.

She was able to sell some of her items directly to the neighborhood's largest store, the Emporium, on a regular basis. That, coupled with her street sales, augmented the family income.

The sun was drowning itself in San Francisco Bay, dying in reflected hues of blood-red, orange and gold. Time to close up. With plans for the evening to look forward to, Star began wrapping and folding and packing the remainder of her goods for the trip home.

"Easy, there, lady, kindly don't be so quick to put stuff away."

Near the wagon stood a man, barely out of adolescence, dressed in cowboy gear. Clearly, he was togged out in his best to impress the sweet young thing clinging to his arm like a limpet.

"We was just wonderin', ma'am," he went on, doffing his rather tattered sombrero, "if you might have any jewelry purty 'nuff to match my Abigail here, in looks."

"Oh, you shush, now, Clint," said Abigail, blushing. And then hissed from the side of her lovely rosebud mouth, "But she's a— she's a—"

"I am, indeed," Star assured the girl without even the smallest loss of her merchant's smile. An encompassing, sympathetic look for the couple, from one to the other. "Something—ah—of substance?"

The cowboy was grinning ear to ear. "Yes, ma'am. Show her, Abby."

Thus entailed, and blushing even more furiously, Abigail extended her left hand to display a modest silver ring encircling the fourth finger. "We're newlyweds," she murmured.

"Yes, ma'am," proclaimed Clint proudly, glancing down at his little bride with an expression of such blazing happiness that Star, taken aback, caught her breath. "Just a little while ago. This is Mrs. Clint Roscoe, and we're headin' on back out to the ranch where I work, in a few minutes. But I saw your cart here, and I thought…"

"Of course you did. And you'd be right. You want a special piece for your beautiful wife. And I have exactly the thing." Turning to the small wagon, with its load of wrapped and folded merchandise, she moved several items here and there. "Let me see. I know there's—ah, here it is."

Carefully removed from its brown paper package, a long silver chain, links glinting in the sunlight, lay draped across her open palms. The accompanying attached pendant glowed with all the fiery iridescent colors of a Mexican opal.

Abigail was staring at the unique work of art with an almost comical mixture of awe and desire. "Oh, Clint," she breathed, enraptured.

"Yes, Abby," Clint agreed with her reaction if not her words. He swallowed hard and then asked, nervously and tentatively, "And—uh—how much would you be askin' for that, ma'am?"

With an empathetic smile, Star stepped forward to slip her necklace over the girl's blonde head and down, where it hung, just below her collar bone, shimmering and shining with every beat of her heart.

"Congratulations, Mr. and Mrs. Roscoe," she told them. "Consider this my wedding gift to you."

Two voices burst out simultaneously: "But we can't take—" and "Oh, I love it, thank you!"

Before she realized what was happening, Star felt herself being enveloped in a monster hug from the bridal couple that ruffled her braids, entangled her turquoise earrings, and shut off her breath. After a minute or two laughing, everyone disengaged and smoothed disrupted things into place.

The young man extended his hand for a hearty shake. "Ma'am, thank you. Thank you heaps," he said fervently. "I dunno what we done to deserve this, but I wanna tell you—we appreciate it more'n you'll ever know."

"Be happy," said Star quietly. "There's little enough happiness in this world, and I'm glad to see yours. So, just—be happy."

It was with a very light heart and quickened step that she finished packing the rest of her goods, hitched up Ezekiel, the mule, and started on her way home. With soft twilight beginning to cast long shadows, and a couple of early stars peeking above the violet horizon, homeowners and shopkeepers alike had lit lamps, closed doors and drawn curtains in preparation for full night.

Normally so self-sufficient and a world unto herself, Star felt a stirring of loneliness as she freed Ezekiel into his small grassy corral and bolted the shed door upon her loaded wagon. Perhaps it was the soulful tune of a harmonica being played somewhere down the street. Perhaps it was the homely whiff of smoke from someone's cook fire.

More likely, she realized, fitting her key into the lock and entering her two-room cabin, it was because loneliness came from— what else?—being alone. Her house sat empty, with no one to greet or be greeted; her life stood empty, with no one to share the smallest happenings or the most eventful of incidents. Maybe she should consider adopting a dog.

It was easier to throw off such disquieting thoughts when the prospect of dinner with friends waited. Hastily stripping down to her undies, she performed a quick sponge bath with her favorite scented soap and then slipped into something feminine and frothy—a white short-sleeved low-cut blouse and its matching full skirt of rich raspberry hue. Black buckle-strapped slippers and a slender necklace of garnet stone completed her costume.

A twirl in front of the mirror assured her that, so dressed, she might mingle in any pureblood haut monde crowd. For the most part—other than occasional childhood confrontations, and, more rarely, an adult slur flung in a hiss or a snarl—she had been able to rise above any feelings of inadequacy about her mestizo background. She had grown up tough, strong, capable, and independent.

Just what the land of sunshine and honey demanded of its citizens.

It would be a short, easy stroll to the Goddard residence. Collecting her sheer lacy black shawl and black silk reticule, Star emerged into an evening scented by evergreen and fern, colored by bayside dusk and touched by a scintillation of fireflies gliding from bush to bush.

San Francisco, soon to be known as the Paris of the West, was a city constantly reinventing itself. From the initial discovery of gold in 1848 to its growing pains of chaotic social climate to the cholera epidemic that resulted in the establishment of the county's first hospital, massive expansion had begun to take place. New buildings in new neighborhoods would appear almost overnight, with sawing and hammering sometimes going on for all hours till next morning.

"Energy" might have been its watchword. And "Vitality" another.

Along with the boom in population, however, also came graft and corruption and a large collection of the lawless element. Sheriff Goddard and his three deputies had their hands full just keeping the streets safe for honest folk.

"Good evenin', Star," said the sheriff at that very moment from his seat on the front porch, as she opened the gate and started up the walkway. "My, my, ain't you lookin' mighty pretty." He turned to his companion to invite a similar compliment, "Don't you agree with me, Matt?"

"I most certainly do." At her approach, Matthew rose to his feet in an immediate display of nice manners. "Mighty pretty." A compliment confirmed by the warmth and approval in his dark eyes.

"Hey, Miss Mendoza." Rob looked up, smiling, from the checkerboard set up on a small table between him and his father. "We're playin'. I'm winnin'."

Star returned the smile, surprised but pleased by the feeling of comfort and security emanating forth. A lonely woman could bask in it. "I'll bet you are, Rob. Something tells me you win most of your games."

"Yeah, he's a crackerjack," said Matt with understandable pride. "I'm thinkin' we'll have to move on to chess soon enough. Will you join us out here for a while, Miss Mendoza?"

"Well, I—thank you, but perhaps later." Oddly flustered, her voice trailed away; and, as she took a first step up, the tight-fitting high-heeled shoes deliberately tried to turn her ankle. Damned white man invention. "I'll—uh—I'll just go inside for now and–um—say hello."

A murmur of conversation led her straight through the parlor to the kitchen, where both women were enjoying a cup of coffee while putting the final touches on tonight's meal. "Oh, hello, my dear," Frances said cheerfully, coming forward. "I'm so glad you were able to be with us, even if this was a spur of the moment affair. Would you like something to drink?"

"Just a glass of water, if you wouldn't mind. Is there something I can do to help?"

"Not a thing, Star. You're our guest, and you've worked all day. So you just sit down and relax while we finish up. Did that nasty old toad Franklin Bower show up again after we left you?"

Happy to comply, Star laughed as she took a chair in the corner. "No, things were quiet. Miss Goddard, I wasn't able to prepare anything to add to tonight's supper, so I hope you will accept this, instead." From out of the reticule came something rough and heavy, then onto the table to be admired.

Sarah, turning from the stove, caught her breath in amazement. "Why, Miss Mendoza. That's a nugget of pure amber. How absolutely beautiful."

"Wherever did you come upon that?" Frances wanted to know. She had picked it up to hold against the waning outdoor light, and now it lay, like a living, vibrating animate object, in her palm.

"Before he traveled to this area and met my mother," Star explained, "my father did some mining in southern California. He found this. The piece is rather spectacular, isn't it?"

"It is, Star. Wondrously so. But surely you don't mean to give it to me."

"I certainly do. Well—to you and the sheriff jointly, I suppose. Miss Goddard." Star gathered her thoughts and then explained, straightforwardly as always. "You've always been so kind to me. You've watched over me, here in town, when my own parents haven't been able to. I would like to repay that kindness a little, if I could. And this seemed to be something you might like."

On an impulse, Frances bent down to pull the girl into her embrace for a sentimental and affectionate hug. It was returned full force. "Thank you, Star. Although it isn't ever necessary for you to think about repayment. But I love this chunk of molten rock you've given me. I shall treasure it, always, knowing it came from you."

"And it's the exact color of her eyes," said Sarah brightly.

The meal was served in the expansive alcove next to the kitchen used as a dining room. Framed pictures of California scenery—the rugged mountains, a brilliant blaze of poppies, someone fishing off a pier—decorated the walls, which had been papered in soft soothing cream and gold; and a brass chandelier had been lighted to cast warmth and radiance over all.

Looking back from far into the future, Star would forever remember this time, this place and these generous friends who had welcomed her into their lives. It was a happy, convivial evening, with plenty of spritely conversation and spontaneous bubbles of laughter. The beef roast, prepared so ably by Frances, had been cooked to perfection: tender, juicy, and spiced with just the right combination of condiments. The accompanying vegetables and flaky rolls disappeared within minutes. The gooey chocolate cake was—well, what can anyone say about chocolate cake, other than it tasting like the fare of angels?

There were a few minor mishaps.

At one point, excitable Rob accidentally tipped over his glass of milk. "No harm done," Frances, well accustomed to children's antics, insisted as she reached for a towel.

At another, a serving bowl of cooked turnips missed its mark in being passed and skittered across the table top to plop itself, upside down, on the floor. "We need a dog," observed Frances, watching William bend over to clean up the mess.

"A dog wouldn't eat this," scoffed her brother. "I'm glad they went. I hate cooked turnips."

At a third, the sheriff made casual reference to the war currently raging across the eastern half of the United States, and its consequences, which ignited a spirited pro and con discussion. Eventually Frances, having had enough as hostess, shut the whole thing down by mention of the ladies' earlier shopping expedition, and their successful hunt for a becoming new hat.

"Oh, 'zat what you called that thing you had on your head," commented William comfortably,
"—becomin'."

Frances threw the damp dish towel at him.

All in all, a successful get-together; and at the end, as plates were being scraped clean of frosting and crumbs, Star looked around at this group of folks she was beginning to consider her in-town family with a great sense of satisfaction and well-being. Smiling, she sighed.

Matthew, across the table, caught the small sound and, immediately understanding, returned the smile. "Nice, huh?"

Her amber eyes met his straight on, with what a scholar might call joie de vivre. "Very nice. The best. Please tell me, Mr. Yancey, how your brother and his new wife are faring. They've taken up residence in town?"

The question was simple enough. The problem was his own distraction.

Because the overhead lamplight was shining down on the glossy black hair, coiled now into a thick knot at the back of her neck, that simply begged to be released into a fall around her shoulders. Whose rounded smoothness, with just a hint of muscle, had been bared by the offset short sleeves.

As for the cleavage given to view, with ripe fullness and umber shadows galore…Matt's mouth suddenly went dry in a spark of pure lust. When had *that* last happened? Too long ago to remember.

"Mr. Yancey?"

His glass of water, hastily sipped, lubricated tongue and loosened tight-set jaw. "Uh—yes, Miss Mendoza. My apologies…just thinkin'—" *Of things you had no right to be thinking, numbskull. You're no better than that libertine, Franklin Bower.* "Well, uh, my new sister-in-law is a teacher, just like Frannie here. A private academy for girls. So, nothin' bein' in session for a while, the two of 'em headed back east by clipper."

"Oh, really?" Frances followed up. "A honeymoon trip?"

"Yes, ma'am. And they'll be closin' up John's Pinkerton business in Boston, and gettin' all his personal stuff packed away for travel. They plan to stay on here, build their lives in San Francisco."

"They got their roots started, all right," agreed William. "They're a grand pair. So's the other newlywed couple, that Bridget and her man, Maximilian Shaw. Wonderful additions to the city. And Miss Cecelia's mentor, Gabe Finnegan, is a damn fine lawyer. I do like that man's style."

Frances handed over the tray of rolls and a small bowl of butter to anyone who wanted more. "Gabe is stepping out with someone, isn't he? I've forgotten just who…"

An affectionate glance from her brother, with a dash of teasing thrown in. "Why, land's sake, Frannie, you old matchmaker. And here it was *you* brought 'em together. Pensacola Rush, her name is—that lady from Philadelphia."

"Well." Bridling like an offended adolescent, she sniffed. "I can't be expected to remember *everyone* I've gotten together. There are simply too many unattached men and women in this city. Which reminds me." A shift toward her friend, and a beguiling smile. "Sarah. We have to talk. I want to find out if you would be interested in—?"

Afterward, the males adjourned to their favorite haunt on the front porch. The youngest, yawning by now, went back to his checkerboard; the two adults settled down, content with one cheroot each, a small tumbler of bourbon, and further discussion about the war, unhampered by the more tender reactions from inside the house.

Where cleanup and organization were proceeding efficiently, with dispatch, directed by Frances. Her kitchen, after all; her rules.

"And what are your plans for the next few days, Star?" Frances, setting a stack of hot freshly dried plates on the cupboard shelf, asked curiously.

Unself-consciously, the girl stretched in a luxurious span of tissue and sinew that lifted both breasts high and full, as enchanting as a mermaid's pose in the role of ship's figurehead. Frances frowned. Now, why couldn't she have presented that image while Matt was still in the room?

No, probably not comfortable enough to do so in his presence. Over the years, Star had had to deal with her share of problems concerning male attention—wanted or not. Why would she think the darkly attractive Texas Ranger might be any different from the others?

"Well, I do need to go visit my parents," she considered, after a minute. "It's been several weeks since I've seen them."

"And you need to replenish your store of merchandise?"

"That and I want to make sure everything is all right. They live in such an isolated area, and I have no way of communication."

Sarah had finished clearing off the table and washing down counters. "Pony Express, perhaps?" she suggested.

"Perhaps. If I could persuade them to establish a route north, instead of south and east." Chuckling, Star rose and began to gather her things together. "Miss Goddard—Frances…thank you for a lovely evening, but I'm afraid I must bring my part of it to an end."

"Of course, I quite understand. It is getting late. Let me just walk you to the door. Sarah?"

"Yes, Frannie. Time for me to leave, too. That little boy must be about asleep in his chair, by now, and we need to get him into his own bed."

Inside every quiet, unassuming teacher resides a bit of the military general. Within jig time, Frances had surveyed the terrain, marshaled her troops, and handed down orders.

"Will, please hitch up the buggy and take Sarah and Rob back to their home. No, we're not about to let them roam around unescorted at this hour of the night. Matthew, be so kind as to escort Miss Mendoza to her home. The same holds true. Oh, stop shilly-shallying, William. You can finish your liquor once you return."

There. Everyone was clearing out, paired up exactly as she had planned, without too much argument...although Star was wearing an uncertain, somewhat mutinous expression. No matter. Frances felt like rubbing her hands together with glee. Except that would be neither ladylike nor professorial.

Chapter 4

"May I assist you with your wrap?" Matt asked attentively, as he paused with Star at the front gate.

"I am certainly able to—I mean…uh…yes, of course, Mr. Yancey. That would be very—" *Forward? Self-serving? Appreciated?* "—uh…helpful."

In the friendly darkness, Matt smiled. Opening the shawl to its full width, he swathed its folds around her, allowing his hands to slip down over her upper arms to smooth every fold in place. "Not much to it, is there?" he observed whimsically. "Sorta like puttin' on a piece of fishnet."

Unconsciously wielding the full effect of her amber eyes as she looked back over her shoulder, she reminded him that the piece was worn more for decorative purpose than for any need to keep warm.

"Ah. I can understand that reasonin'. Otherwise, I think you'd be better off coverin' up with a blanket." *Or with me. Snuggled up close and tight, I'd keep you warm. Maybe even make you warmer.*

Looking down from all his rangy height, past the back of her head into the temptation of her bare cleavage, within easy reach and just begging to be caressed, had about driven him around the bend. What the hell was going on here? He was acting like a moonstruck kid, half-crazed for a quick roll in the hay.

Not that he would, for God's sake. He would neither discredit his wife's memory nor disgrace this girl he was honor-bound to treat with dignity and respect, seeing her safely home to her own quarters.

What kind of devil would he be, anyway, if the danger he meant to protect her from was himself?

His jaw set tight again, against blurting out things he shouldn't even be thinking; a mental gate slammed shut, against the rising of emotion and of parts stirred up, taking notice, demanding service. Awkward moving, in such a situation, especially during an evening jaunt, but he'd manage somehow.

"Well, we'd best be headin' along," Matt informed his companion stiffly. "At this rate it'll be midnight b'fore you get back."

"All right," she agreed equably. "This way, please."

Frances had provided them with a lantern, which he was swinging loose on his left side. His right arm had been crooked at the elbow, giving Star the support she might need for striding over any rough, uneven spots in the walkway. He must admit, though, he was enjoying the feel of her hand curled around his bicep.

Damn. There he was, again, despite all his resolutions!

"How'dja come to be called Star?" he asked on a surge of desperation. Talk, talk, talk; anything to get his mind up on the level it should be, instead of hovering low, around physical need.

"Goldenstar, actually." She peered up at him with a smile. "It's a shrub that grows here in the state. A ground cover. My mother was quite taken with both the color and the name. So. Here I am."

"Pretty. Any kinda smell to that flower?"

Under the lacy shawl she shrugged. "Smell? Green, I suppose. Like any plant. Why do you ask?"

"Well, it's just—I like whatever perfume you're wearin'. Light. Sweet. Thought maybe that was related to the goldenstar."

Another pedestrian out for his evening constitutional approached, tipped his hat, swerved around to the other side, and kept briskly on. The heavy tread stirred up an entire performing musicale of crickets and a light brigade of fireflies.

"We turn here at the corner," Star reported. "And how did you come to be called Matthew?"

"Matthew? Guess it was just my ma's choice for—oh. Nothin' outa the way, like yours. So you're joshin' me."

Her eyes crinkled with amusement. "I am, indeed, Mr. Yancey. Just a little."

"Huh."

Into the next block, and then another, one short, one long. Celebratory noise drifted up the famous hills toward them, with laughter and the shouts of children and even a gunshot or two. "Somebody must be havin' a birthday party," Matt observed, pausing to listen. And to avoid any stray bullets.

"Don't you just love this time of the day?" Star murmured, sniffing deeply of the night air and all its interesting odors. Some quite pleasant, some not so much. "The work is done, the trouble is past, and it's time just to sit and rock a spell."

"Well, yeah, if all that is true. Here, careful, there's a tree root stickin' right outa the ground." Distracted, he guided her past the obstacle, then resumed, "I useta feel that way on the plantation. Belle Clare, near Charleston. Nice quiet evenin', maybe some friends over to do some visitin', maybe just sittin' down somewhere by yourself."

"You grew up there."

"Yes, ma'am. Then after Paw died, we boys got together and sold the homestead, years before the war started. Figured it was the most prudent thing t'do. None of us wanted to get caught up in the storm clouds we saw comin'."

"And you miss it?"

He looked off into the distance, where bay water reflected the yellow glow of ship lights, and even from here a ruckus at various saloons could be seen and heard. "On bad days, I miss it," he admitted in a low voice. "What we used to have. Luxury. Comfort. Security. Not so much of that, once you move out into the world. As you prob'ly know, Miss Mendoza. And maybe some of what I miss is just plain nostalgia. But life is a challenge. You meet it and win, or you die."

Star shivered a little. "That sounds terribly gloomy."

"After my wife died, and then my father, and then we sold the home place, I was chock full of gloom and doom for a good long while. But that eased up a bit, once the boy started needin' my attention."

"You're a lucky man there, Matthew Yancey," she pointed out. As if any reminder was really necessary! "Rob is a wonderful child, and the two of you seem to be very close."

"He brought me through the worst," said Matt frankly. "And not even aware he was keepin' me goin'. But that's kids, ain't it? Most of 'em are happy-go-lucky little devils."

She laughed. "I do see that in him. Here, Mr. Yancey. This is my house."

Lifting his lantern high as they approached, Matt surveyed the small cabin with approval. A wide front porch, two handmade twig chairs made comfortable by cushions, planter boxes stuffed full of native plants—several types of sage, bright orange poppy, mint, and her own goldenstar—offered welcome. As did a colorful rag rug and equally colorful curtains at the double windows.

"Snug," was his reaction. "And cozy."

"If cozy means small, then certainly cozy. But it suits me." Pulling a key from her reticule, Star unlocked her door and paused, feeling suddenly uncertain and a little shy. "Thank you for walking me home, Mr. Yancey. I appreciate your consideration."

He set his lantern down on the railing, carefully balanced, to tuck one shoulder against the door jamb. "Well, I didn't see that I had much choice in the matter," he chuckled. "Given Frannie's insistence on how she was arrangin' things. But, Miss Mendoza—Star—" The tone of his voice softened slightly, as he studied her lovely face in the lamplight, "I'd'a done it anyway, Frannie or no Frannie. I—uh—I enjoyed your company."

Earlier, an array of butterflies had taken flight in Star's middle; now the whole flock of them fluttered northward, halting her breath and causing serious seizures with speech. "Oh. Well. Thank you. I—I—it's been a—a very nice evening, Mr. Yancey. Matt."

A lazy lopsided smile sent imps dancing in his dark eyes, and his big body leaned slightly toward her, like a towering ponderosa, standing near. Very near. Too near. She was feeling suffocated by his nearness.

"Star," he whispered. Gray sombrero doffed, his thick black hair tumbled anyhow over his brow, outlining the fine shape of his skull and the intricate curve of his ears.

He raised his right hand to slant along the side of her jaw, holding her in place, while his thumb slipped slowly, carefully, back and forth across the fullness of her lower lip. An incredibly erotic bit of play that roused all the senses and begged for more.

In one convulsive movement she managed to swallow. Trembling, she tried to shift position but was trapped by the wall behind her. "I think you—I think this—you—"

"Sssshhh."

With that, he bent forward and covered her quivering mouth with his own. Gently at first, then, as desire rose, more urgently, with all the power and force of a passionate man.

For a few delightful minutes Star succumbed. She even raised up, midway through that life-taking kiss, to mesh her fingers into his hair, to tug him closer into the embrace.

Matt was lost. His hat got thrown aside, somewhere along the way; his hand plunged downward over her throat and around her breast with rough need; his knee came up slightly, entangled in the volume of her skirts in tandem with anything else seeking entrance. A smothered sound, almost a growl, escaped him.

That was when she suddenly came to herself.

"No." She had pulled free enough to gasp a protest. "No. Let me go!"

"Star—" Deaf and blind to all but his own intent, Matt was snatching hungry little kisses from her cheek, her earlobe, the thundering pulse at her collar bone.

"Stop it!" Furious, she kicked out at him in a whirl of raspberry chintz. "How dare you treat me this way?"

Finally, through a flood of rampaging testosterone and blood-red mist, that reached him. Stunned, he released his grip and took a slow step backward.

"You think you can behave toward me as do so many other men in this town?" she spat out at him, hurt and angry all at once. "You think you can cheapen me, degrade me, just because I am mestizo? You think I count for nothing?"

Ice water filled his veins. "Star. Miss Mendoza. Please, I am—I am terribly sorry. You're right, I shouldn'ta—"

"We met for the first time this morning," she rushed on over a sob. "Just this morning. And you are already trying to—trying to cozen me into—"

"I didn't mean—" Matt began miserably.

"Ah, of course you did! Go away, Matthew Yancey. Go away. Your charming southern boy manners are all—just an act, to—to deceive—" The tears were falling in a storm surge by then. Rather than let him witness any more of her humiliation, Star fumbled with the handle, flung herself inside, and slammed the solid door shut behind her.

"I'm sorry," Matt whispered again to the empty air. "I am so goddamned sorry."

Deeply ashamed, he bent down to retrieve his hat with the stiffened, palsied movements of an arthritic old man. How could such a bright, entertaining evening have turned into such a disaster?

The lantern was still burning with a steady flame. Hoisting the handle, he stepped down from Star's front porch and turned away. Just as he had been ordered.

Chapter 5

Damn it. Franklin Bower opened one eye to survey his surroundings.

A stench wafting in from the kitchen made it clear his cook had burned another breakfast. Probably a damned costly cut of steak, too. Time to boot her out of his house and off the ranch. She knew no more about preparing American food than she knew about governing the State of California, for God's sake. Too bad if she was old and needed the salary, meager though it was. Let her take up begging on the streets of San Francisco for a while. Serve her right.

Damn it. He opened the other eye.

The little strumpet in the bed beside him had not only rolled herself up into the only blanket, but she'd taken both of his pillows besides. Time to boot her out, too.

"Raquel. Raquel!" He stretched one leg across the mattress to kick at the girl's naked and oblivious backside. "Move your lazy ass, girl."

"Uhhhh…Whassamatter, señor…?" She shifted, scrubbed at her sleepy face, and yawned. "You wanna make love 'gain?"

"Hell, no," snorted Bower. "I'm done with you. Go on, get up and out. Find yourself some other pigsty to lay in."

Pouting, Raquel sat up and turned toward him, offering a full view of her lush, caramel-tipped breasts. Even this morning, after a night of being roughly and badly used, her rather common prettiness shone through the bruises. "You don' want me no more, señor?" she tried again.

"What, are you deaf as well as blind?" Bower snarled. He aimed another kick in her direction that toppled her onto the floor with a crash. "Get out. And take all your slop with you!"

Tears would hold no sway with the tyrannical boss-man, nor would pleas for mercy. Resigned to whatever outcome an unkind fate might deal her, Raquel gathered up her clothing and slunk away.

Bower hauled his own naked body out of bed, stretched, scratched, and stretched some more. Last night's wine had left a sour taste in his mouth. As had the violent intervals of sex. In reality, a half-witted servant girl had provided an outlet for his appetites; in fantasy, it was Star Mendoza who lay under him, moaning with supposed pleasure and responding to every maneuver.

Time to make that fantasy into reality.

"Horace!" he shouted, reaching for a robe. "Fill my tub. And then go get me a tray with somethin' decent to eat. I gotta clean up and get to town."

A down-on-his-luck former manservant for a visiting British duke, Horace had accepted the position at Franklin Bower's ranch out of desperation. Truth to tell, he hated this Condor place and its despicable owner almost as much as he hated the whole state of California and its hot, dry climate. Had he and his onetime employer not parted company for the most trivial of reasons, he would still be happily plying his trade in foggy London, even now.

"Shall you be wanting a particular suit, Mr. Bower?" Horace asked in plummy tones.

"Yeah, I'll pick one after I'm done here. This water ain't very damned hot."

"My apologies, sir. Would you like me to add more?"

"Naw." The slam of a door, more grumbling, and a splash. "Go get me some food, Horace," came racketing from the closed bathroom. "I've had a hard night and I'm hungry. And be quick about it."

Freshly bathed and shaved, his mustache trimmed, his coarse black hair combed back, and his favorite gray suit nicely pressed, he paused to preen in front of the bedroom mirror. Damn, but he was a fine figure of a man. Rich, too; and getting richer every day. What could Goldenstar Mendoza possibly not like about him?

Feeling as cocky as some puffed-up rooster in a crowded henhouse, he made his way to the dining room. Palatial. Downright palatial, with its thick carpets and exotic woods and gold-trimmed table service. He'd sunk a good deal of money into the furbishing of this cavernous ranch house, all with an eye toward the effect such luxury would have on the woman he intended to install here. Would she be impressed? Would she appreciate his effort? Would she settle in and take advantage of everything he had provided?

Bower seated himself at the expansive table, gobbling down buttered bread and scrambled eggs while perusing his most recent copy of The Daily Evening Bulletin. Partway through, he shouted for his manservant once more.

"Something I can do for you, sir?" Horace glided into the room to ask smoothly.

"More coffee. Hot this time. And then have Tomás hitch up the buggy for me. I'm leavin' soon."

Not soon enough, thought Horace resentfully, gliding away.

It was a lovely morning, with enough early sunlight to splash through the leafy branches of ficus and oak and red-flowering gum blossoms. Even here, a very faint whiff of salt air mingled with the scent of powder-dry dust underfoot and the tang of evergreen swept down from the hills. One bird called to another, off in the distance, and overhead a Cooper's hawk swooped and dipped across the cloudless sky.

But Franklin, careening along toward the city in his springy Eureka carriage, was mentally reviewing plans for the day. He had neither time for, nor interest in, scenery. Given opportunity, he would cheerfully flatten everything if his Condor Ranch could just be expanded by another million acres or so. In another era, he might be considered a pillager of ethical standards, an environmental polluter, a toxic waste dump in the making.

For now, he was merely greedy, fiercely ambitious, belligerent, and aggressive as a wolverine.

Arriving a little later at his first stop, he climbed down, tied the mare to a hitching post, and clumped his way into Hanrahan's Saloon. Probably too early for a good stiff drink. Still, maybe one little nip would help strengthen his resolve and settle his roiled stomach. Why not a chaser after those godawful breakfast eggs?

"Back in town so soon?"

A sip of the bartender's premium whiskey before a slow sideways turn of the head. "H'lo, Sykes. Buy you a drink?"

Grinning, Russell Sykes reached out to hook a chair leg with the heel of his boot. "Me, I never say no to an offer like that. Thanks. You're well turned out this mornin', Franklin."

Bower glanced down at his dark-gray pinstriped suit, still almost as fresh as when he'd buttoned himself into it a few hours ago. "Yeah, got some business to transact. How's that whiskey tastin', there, Russell?"

"Oh, fine. Mighty fine." To prove it, he emptied his shot glass and reached out for the bottle to pour another.

Much more prudent to merely sip the stuff, if you wanted to keep a clear head about you. "You find yourself a job yet?"

"A job? Hell, no, I ain't found a job yet. Christ in a handcart, I only just saw you in here yesterday. Where d'you think I'd find a job that quick?"

"Well, I don't rightly know, since I ain't the one lookin' for work." Another slow sip. Not the best he'd ever had, but getting better by the minute. "Howsoever, somethin's come up that I might need some help with. You interested?"

"Damn straight I'm interested." Sykes leaned in from his chair, ostensibly to listen attentively but also to pour out one more generous helping. "Whatcha got in mind?"

The man's forward lean sent Bower leaning back. Sykes badly needed a bath. And a shampoo. And maybe a dash of eau de cologne. "Well, now," drawled the rancher, "I got somethin' goin' on that I wanna take care of. And I may want you around for backup. So here's the plan."

* * * * * * * * * * * * * * * *

Long, lost, lonely night hours, given over to spasmodic periods of weeping, interspersed with spasmodic periods of resignation and depression, interspersed with more spasmodic periods of weeping. Somehow the minutes had ticked past, from full dark to early dawn, offering little surcease from the rant of recriminations chasing round and round inside her weary brain.

And all because, after living a lifestyle unencumbered and independent, she had fallen in love with a tall, bodacious Texas Ranger who had treated her like a bought-and-paid-for woman of the streets.

In all honesty, she probably had only herself to blame. What else could he have thought, given her response to his oh so delightful overtures?

She'd been caught at a weak and vulnerable moment. And had paid for it.

How would she dare look at him, even speak to him again, after such shameful behavior? Were her mother to hear of it, she would worriedly counsel patience and forbearance; her father would quietly load his gun.

At sunrise Star finally dragged her aching, exhausted body from bed. No point in trying to wring any more sleep from a sleepless position. Padding barefoot out to the kitchen / living area, she collected a small armful of kindling from its basket beside the back door, to revive the cook stove's banked fire.

Crackling flames and a filled coffeepot set on to boil meant a resurgence of energy, if not a lifting of low spirits. A cool wet cloth pressed to swollen eyes and fevered face helped ease physical discomfort. Easing the discomfort of a prickled conscience and a troubled heart would take more. Was an experience like this what drove men to seek the solace of firewater?

Better days would come along. Everything happened for a reason. She would emerge on the other side of the tunnel, stronger than ever.

How many of her father's old family proverbs had she heard and absorbed? How many did she still believe held true? Difficult to return to logic and philosophical reasoning when her mood was so bleak!

For a while she simply sat at her plain wooden table, sipping the hot hardy brew and contemplating life in general, her own in particular, as the morning moved on around her.

Lofty alder and poplar trees shaded her modest home from the worst of summer sun; their overhanging branches now sheltered a bevy of birds, trilling and cooing, mating and fighting, rustling in the leaves. Off in the distance a dog barked, then another joined in. Someone way down the street could be heard whistling tunelessly.

Sighing, Star glanced at her little clock ticking the seconds away from the corner what-not shelf. Breakfast first: one of yesterday's corn muffins from the pantry. Then a bath. Then a trip with Ezekiel to the high hills of her family. When the world crashed, when disaster portended, when sanity descended into chaos, only Adsila Mendoza could make things right again.

Her painted tin tub might be neither large nor elaborate, but it served her needs; and the cook stove's reservoir provided just enough warm water. A small capful of precious scented oil added the finishing touch. Soap. Towel. Another cup of coffee. Fresh underwear at the ready. Long heavy hair pulled up and fastened into a knot.

Stripping out of her muslin nightgown right down to her altogethers, Star stepped into the bath and sank back with one more heartfelt sigh. If life had recently beaten you up, almost past bearing, this type of leisurely soak could offer a soothing panacea.

Time, in all its dispassionate silence, passed on. A few beads of water dripped off the tub's rim and onto the wooden floor. Plop. Plop. Plop. Lazily, luxuriously, Star squeezed a sponge over one arm, then the other.

Peace. Quiet. After the storm, the calm.

Thump! Thump!

"Oh!" Startled by the loud, demanding knock on her front door, she dropped the sponge and jerked upright. No one ever came to visit her. No one ever wanted in. If she stayed silent and unmoving, perhaps the caller would assume the house to be empty and go away.

Thump! Thump!

"Star! I know you're in there. Your damn mule is still out in the corral, eatin' his fool head off. C'mon, answer the door."

The shades attached to both bedroom windows had been carefully pulled all the way down, to the sill. Privacy and seclusion she had expected to have in abundance. Apparently not so. The rancher must have a nose like a ferret, to track her down and corner her so easily.

Thump! Thump!

"C'mon, Star, dammit, open the goddamned door! Lissen, I got people here. I'll break it down if I have to."

On the bedside table, within easy reach, lay her Colt 1860 Army Revolver, presented with great ceremony and solemnity by Daniel, upon achieving the move to town. Six shots. Loaded and primed and ready to use. But did she dare?

A couple of hard kicks aimed at the door, none too sturdy to begin with. How much longer would it hold together?

By now, sharply awake and every sense cued to danger, like a hunted prey driven to lair, Star had eased from the tub, quickly toweled dry, and quickly pulled on underthings, a simple white blouse, a full black skirt, and her favorite moccasins.

If Bower broke into her home, and she shot him for it, Star knew just exactly what she could expect for punishment. Consider the outrage: a white man—attacked by a mestizo? At the very least, riots, mobs, imprisonment; at the worst, death by hanging.

Reluctantly putting aside any hope of self-defense, she cast a last lingering look at the charged weapon and turned away.

But she would not go down completely helpless and unprotected. Right foot propped on a stool, skirt pulled aside, Star hastily wrapped and tied the thong of her sheathed knife around the middle of her upper thigh. Not only did she know how to attach it, she knew how to use it. And damned well, too. Not for nothing did her veins run with Cherokee blood.

"Star! Are you comin' out, or am I comin' in?"

"What do you want, Franklin Bower?"

"Ha." A lewd chuckle from the other side of the door. At least the banging had stopped. "I knew you were in there, girl. I can smell you."

"Then you have the better of me. You are invading the privacy of my home Mr. Bower, and I have a gun aimed right about where you are standing." Courageous and resolute though she might appear, her insides were quaking. Only now, in this cabin situated on the edge of town, was she realizing how far distant the rest of humanity lay. "So, I repeat, what do you want?"

A slight drum of fingers on the doorframe. Teasing. "What I've always wanted, Star," came the low, insinuating voice. "You."

"Go away, Mr. Bower. Leave now and I won't press charges against you."

"Press charges!" He laughed. A hyena's baying laugh. "Oh, you do amuse me, Miss Mendoza. I look forward to some interestin' times, you and me. Now, we're still standin' here talkin', with a door between us. How about you open up? In more ways than one."

Shaken and sickened, with bile rising in her throat, she shifted from one foot to the other. Escape. Escape how? Front door blocked, back door nonexistent; from a window? Could she possibly open a window without drawing attention, slip out and through and away?

"Oh, I toldja I got people here, Star. Watchin'. No way t' get free but through me. So, whaddya say, you gonna behave yourself and c'mon? I got big plans for us there at the ranch. It'll be easy livin' for you—nothin' to do but pleasure me."

Star nearly gagged. "I'd rather kiss a snake!" she spat.

"Yeah? Not very refined, now, are you? Well, see, here's the thing." A rustle of cloth as he leaned comfortably against the cabin's outside wall, prepared to stay for however long it took to dislodge her into his possession. "I know all about your maw, Star. I know why she hides out in the hills."

Silence. She had gone cold all over, and goose bumps covered her bare arms.

"It happened a long time ago, didn't it? But I know the whole story. Man, and what a story it was." That lewd chuckle again. Salacious. Vulgar. "Got herself attacked by a white man, so I heard. Nothin' serious, just wantin' a little nookie. But she knifed the poor bastard. Nearly did him in."

She could not breathe. She could not, to save her soul, catch a breath.

"Yep. Bad wound. He finally recovered, but she skedaddled b'fore anybody found out who did it." Casually, "Got a price on her head, don't she? Be a real shame if that sheriff friend of yours found out where she's livin', had to haul her back t'town in handcuffs. Wouldn't it, Star? Wouldn't that be a real shame?"

Only a few yards away from him, inside her parlor, she was staring at the closed and barred front door as if it were some terrible red-eyed beast about to attack. Then suddenly a wrench of pain straight through her middle, like the gut of a knife blade, doubled her over.

"Yes, sir," went on the unctuous voice, "got me a real nice carriage waitin' right here, Star, t'take us out to the Condor. All the comforts."

She was trapped, with no way to gain her freedom. This odious man had won. With slow, crabbed movements, she straightened, brushed both hands over her flowing skirts as if to purge herself of accumulated dirt, and took one careful step forward. Then another. And another.

"Well, well," Bower greeted her with a huge grin as she opened the door. "I knew you'd see it my way. Here, let me help you into the surrey. Hey, Sykes," he called to his hired flunky, waiting by his horse, "you can follow me on out. Star and me, we got things t'talk about."

Chapter 6

"Star's late this morning."

"I know." Anxiously, Frances peered up and down the street, looking in vain for a small wagon drawn by an unusually patient long-eared mule. "And she's always so punctual. It isn't like her not to be right on time."

"And didn't we arrange to meet early with her, to find out how things went with Mr. Yancey last night? Young Master Yancey," the housekeeper turned in an aside to her charge, "I know this isn't a lot of fun for you at the moment, but kicking at the tree won't get my attention any faster."

"Aw, gee whiz." Gloomily, Rob shoved his hands into his pockets and cast about for a new activity. "Then how's about I jist head out for a walk by my ownself?"

Sarah sniffed. "That'll be the day. Do you know how many riffraffy types hang around, getting good honest folks into trouble?"

"No," said Rob, brightening. "How many?"

"I have an idea," put in Frances at this point. She bent forward, hands on knees, as if imparting some great secret. "Did you know there's a whole toy section in the Emporium, only begging to be explored? What do you think, shall we go see?"

From bright to beaming, then a nod with gusto. "Ab-so-lute-ly!" he brought that out with pride.

Smiling across at her companion, Frances patted the small boy on his tousled head. "Then absolutely we need to visit there, straightaway."

With Rob skipping happily along several steps ahead—and singing some nonsensical song that earned the smiles of passersby—the two women were able to talk more freely.

"My brother refused to give me any details about last night," Frances began. "Not one word of explanation or description."

"Really?"

"However, he did seem to be extraordinarily *cheerful* this morning. He was actually whistling on his way to the breakfast table. And he took the stairs two at a time."

"Did he?"

"He planned to meet Matthew at the office later on. He was grinning like a Halloween pumpkin when he told me that."

"Was he, now?"

Frances halted short, long enough to stamp her foot in exasperation. "Sarah!"

"Yes?"

The one word response was accompanied by a dimple. Frances nearly dropped her reticule. During the past month of their association, during their times of shared laughter and shared history, Sarah had not produced one dimple. Where had *that* come from?

"Robert Malachai Yancey," Sarah digressed to call ahead, "no further, please. That's plenty far to keep your distance."

"Okay, Mrs. Coleman," he called back, good-humoredly. In form and coloring he was a miniature of his father, already taller than the average child, with an intelligence and acumen surprising for his age. "But you might try keepin' up with me."

Amusement crinkled the housekeeper's faded blue eyes. "Oh, he is a pistol, that one," she murmured. "All right, Frannie. You want to know what happened last night between your brother and me. If anything happened."

"It seems only fair," said Frances tartly, "since I was the only one left home by myself to twiddle my thumbs."

"Spinning your web, more likely. He kissed me."

"Kissed you! Why, Sarah Coleman!"

There, that elusive dimple again. In fact, two of them.

Frances eyed her friend with speculation and curiosity. "And...was it—?"

"It was very nice, Frannie. A very proper kiss good-night. On the cheek." A hint of mischief now in the slanted sideways glance.

"Ah. Well, at least he behaved himself."

"Of course he did. He has his sister's example to follow."

A silent minute ticked by, then another, while they strolled along the wooden walk. In the ongoing city-wide building boom, the distant noise of sawing and hammering was never far distant. Nor was the rattle of passing wagons, loaded to the rims, and the neighing or clomping of draft horses, and the occasional curse or shout of a drover. Some yards away, young Rob had stopped to watch a cart being unpacked of boxes and crates.

"This place never stops growing," observed Frances, who admired such energetic hustle and bustle. "Whether it's improvement or not is open to—"

"He wants to see me again. Just me. Alone. For dinner at the hotel, or a night at the theatre."

A gleeful light broke and slowly spread across her features. "Well, it's about time. Took him long enough." Pausing, she peered at Sarah more intently in an attempt to read her mood. "Sarah. It seemed to me a good match, you and William. You do like him a little, don't you?"

Staring straight ahead, watching the boy who was watching the cart, Sarah murmured, "I do like him. I like him a lot. He's a kind and caring man, with a wonderful sense of humor."

"Well, then." Frances felt inordinately pleased that at least one of her arrangements was working out as she had planned. "He's never married, you know. And it's about time he sets up housekeeping on his own. We get along like oil and vinegar. Here, come join us, Rob. There's the Emporium."

The ladies were standing near the fabric counter, ostensibly looking over dress patterns while keeping a careful eye on Rob in the small toy section, when Frances once again voiced her concerns about Star's nonappearance. Few customers had meandered their way this mid-morning hour, and she able to speak freely.

"It does seem odd that she's nowhere around," Sarah agreed, somewhat distracted.

So many choices: the light green bonnet with a handful of cabbage roses or the flat straw skimmer and its flattering pink bow? What was William's favorite color? Would he notice a new hat, and compliment her on how well it suited her complexion?

Frances had leaned back against the paneled wall, both arms folded across her breast in a very unladylike manner. "She's always in town by now. Something just doesn't feel right, Sarah."

The soft caramel-colored velvet, edged in blue grosgrain ribbon. Definitely that one: a charming and unusual combination. Satisfied by her choice, Sarah sighed and re-directed her attention to what was most pressing. "Didn't she mention a plan to go visit her parents?"

"Yes. But later on...in a few days." Discontent, the teacher glanced about the Emporium's wide variety of merchandise, as if by wishing alone she would see Star suddenly appear. "Besides, we spoke of her walk home, with Matt. I'm so anxious to find out what happened."

A small tow-headed boy about Rob's age had wandered away from his mother to explore whatever toys the establishment might offer. Happily the youngsters were beginning to examine wooden trains, a horse and carriage made of tin, several sets of drums, and an assortment of miniature painted soldiers with their military equipment.

"Do you think she may have met with an accident?" Sarah's tentative utterance echoed the words Frances had not dared speak aloud.

"I don't know. But I do know," she straightened, suddenly filled with purpose and resolve, "that we need to go find William— and Matthew, if the two are together; even if they're busy on another case. Someone with more experience in these matters simply must investigate."

The two certainly were together, but hardly busy. On a good day, an easy day, William could complete paperwork or walk about his town, supervising, to ensure that all was as it should be, while one or two of his deputies handled actual complaints and arrests. At this time, shortly before the late August noon, the sheriff and the Ranger had decided to occupy boardwalk chairs just outside his office door.

Neither had much to say at the moment, despite William's invitation to sit and "chew the fat" for a while. Both were still lost in thought concerning last night's activities.

William's were marvelously optimistic, upbeat, and heartened for the future.

Sarah has such nice blue eyes, with a twinkle that catches your attention, and a kind, gentle, humorous way about her. At least she laughs at my jokes. Not to mention bein' pretty as a painted wagon. And good with kids, too; look at how she takes care of Matt's motherless son, bringin' him up to respect his elders and to look at life just like she does. A feller could do worse. A feller could do a lot worse.

She's—what, maybe mid-thirties? Not too old to remarry and start a family of her own. Me neither, as far as that goes. Hell, I'm only pushin' forty, got a good job and a nice house. Reckon her and me gettin' together—it's somethin' that could happen easy. As long as I don't scare her off. As long as I don't make the wrong moves.

"Think I'll get me a refill on my coffee," William abruptly said into the silence. "How about you, Matt?"

"Sheriff, I toldja before, this stuff tastes about as bad as the inside of a cow. So—no, thanks. One cup a day is all I can deal with."

"Huh. All right, then. Back in a minute."

Which left Matt briefly alone, to think his own thoughts. Not nearly as cheerful as those of his friend. Morbid, in fact; downright depressing.

What the hell did I figure I was doin', treatin' her like that? Just b'cause she's the first woman since Elisa died that I've felt any interest in. Sure, maybe she gave back as good as she got, but that was no reason to let her see just how far I could go. Dammit. Prob'ly spooked her for all and good by now. I should be hawse whipped. Or, at the very least, given a hard kick in the backside.

Should I try seein' her again? Makin' another apology and hopin' she'll listen? Maybe Frannie would take my point of view, help smooth things over. Dammit. Sure would like to make things right. Spend more time together, maybe build a relationship. She's a fine-lookin' woman, with a fine character. And I'm interested. I'm definitely interested. Maybe if I—

"Hello, Matthew."

"Uh." The voice struck right in the middle of his ruminations, like a hammer to an anvil, and Matt was rudely jerked back to reality. Quickly, he surged to his feet, with a tip of his hat. "Good mawnin', Frannie. Mrs. Coleman. Rob. You all been out shoppin' again?"

"Yes, yes, we—well, somewhat. Matt, where is that fool brother of mine?"

"Right here, Frannie," William offered a mild reply to his sister's gibe as he emerged from the shadowed doorway. "What's goin' on? You sound worried."

"Well, I am. We haven't seen or heard from Star today, and it's up to you to find out why."

William blinked. "But, Frannie, we just had supper with her last night. She was fine when Matt walked her home. At least—" He turned in appeal, "—she *was* fine, wasn't she?"

A deep florid blush crawled up from the Ranger's muscular neck into his sunburnt cheeks. "Uh."

"I knew it!" Frances pounced like a hawk with talons extended. "I knew something was wrong. What did you do, Matthew Yancey?"

Matt took a hurried step backward. In Frances Goddard he recognized a fearless foe, one he would be wise not to cross. "Just—uh—I sorta—kissed her good night."

"What else?"

"Aw, c'mon, Frannie," her brother pleaded for restraint. "That ain't the kinda thing you should be askin'. A man likes to keep his lovemakin' private."

In the shade of the shingled canopy overhead, Sarah glanced his way. It needed only her small, significant smile to send a sudden blush rising into the sheriff's features, as well.

"Well, private as can be, anyway," he amended. "So don't you go gettin' all over Matt's case. He done what you asked him; he walked the girl home. How's come you need to know any more details than that?"

"Because something has happened to her, Will," said Frances in low, intense tones. Hands planted firmly on hips, she had backed down from her original warrior's stance but refused to give way completely. "I feel it in my bones. I'm very worried."

For the past several argumentative minutes, Matt had been considering his own role in last night's disastrous encounter, and various outcomes that might have resulted therefrom. Hiding in her cabin, due to emotional hurt, was one possibility; sulking was another; off and about with abject disappointment a third. Or a combination of all three. Who could tell, when it came to dealing with a woman? The thought of foul play as a fourth possibility seemed almost ludicrous.

Now, having reached a decision, he volunteered to go see if she was home. Or if not, whether anyone had a clue as to her whereabouts. And then haul her back here, posthaste, to answer for upsetting her friends. "If that would relieve your distress, Frances," he added politely.

"It would, indeed, Matt. Thank you. I suppose Sarah and I could have done that ourselves, but—"

"But you didn't know exactly what to expect, or how to proceed. I know. Rob, please stay here with Mrs. Coleman till I get back."

"All right, Daddy," nodded the boy. "I gots this stuff to play with, anyway." He extended an armful of treasure, for display: one hand-carved wooden whistle, a spinning top, and several cloth-covered books.

"Good God!" Matt was understandably startled. "Where'dja get all that, son?"

He pointed. "Miss Goddard."

"Frances—"

"I have an account there, it's nothing. Now, do hush and hurry up; you need to see Star. And please bring her along when you return."

"Yes, ma'am." Another touch of fingers to his hat brim, and Matt was hastening away.

Today's walk, taken solo instead of as half of a couple, during bright sunlit hours instead of a dreamy and romantic moon-drenched interval, offered little besides the opportunity for a brisk walk and more contemplation of his wrongs.

Marching along got him to Star's cabin in short time. Reaching it, Matt paused to absorb and appreciate the look of the place, as a whole. Neatly swept, carefully repaired, every detail in good order. As surely it would not be, were there problems.

Still, an air of inordinate quiet lay over all. As if the snug little house were holding its breath, waiting for its owner to return from some other destination.

Matt shook his head. Strange notion, which made no sense.

He climbed the step and knocked at the door. "H'lo, Star?"

Silence. So peculiar a silence, that, if he were a fanciful man, it might be seen as fraught with mystery, or even tragedy. "Star— Miss Mendoza—you in there?"

Another knock, more forceful. And this time the door slowly opened partway, with a soft creak.

Unlocked. Most unusual.

Drawing his Colt revolver from its holster, Matt cautiously pushed in the rest of the way, peering around as he entered. Nothing. Nobody. The cabin's interior of parlor / kitchen presented the same picture of apple-pie order as the outside. Every stick of furniture apparently in place, every incidental of pillow or afghan or rug smooth and unruffled.

"Star?"

Still silence. A heavy, brooding silence.

He moved further into the room, glancing from right to left, then stepped through the open doorway into a bedroom. From there, a light, feminine scent drifted out.

Odd. In the middle of the floor stood a tin tub filled with water, and a crumpled-up towel beside it. Besides that, what proved to be, upon cursory examination, a white muslin night gown. Matt bent to dip a free hand into the water. Cold. Or, if not cold, at least not hot. Room temperature. And the towel held only a faint feel of dampness.

Wherever she had gone, then, it wasn't so very long ago.

From wall to wall, his gaze encompassed the compact space. A couple of paintings here and there, a couple of kerosene lamps whose chimneys stood clean and shining, a couple of throw rugs. A full-sized brass bed, covered with a colorful quilt and several pillows. And, on the small wooden table, a Colt revolver holstered into its gun belt, very like his own. Interesting.

Outdoors once again, he checked the shed. Only Star's wagon there, filled with her stockpile of goods for sale, neatly stored under a canvas cover. Ezekiel plopped his chin onto the top rail of the corral and brayed for attention. Matt paused to rub his ears. Plenty of shade, plenty of water, plenty of grass; the animal was well cared for. Like everything else on Goldenstar's property.

Then where the hell was she?

The tidy aspect of grounds and house—other than those minor forgotten elements pertaining to her bath—pointed to a recent absence. A long walk, perhaps. A cooling-off period.

That could be a positive thing. If she were given time to think things over, it could work to his benefit. She might come to realize that he hadn't meant any disrespect toward her. He'd simply been carried away by her beauty and charm into pushing past accepted boundaries.

Try explaining *that* in a way that sounded sincere!

Meanwhile, he would pull Frances aside for a private talk. Without revealing too much about his own crass behavior, he might be able to pry out some words of advice from the matchmaker herself.

Chapter 7

"This here's the new lady of the house," Franklin introduced her to the staff. "Now, you may notice that she ain't actin' real happy to be with us. But that'll change once she settles in. So I want all of you t' take damn good care of her."

Endurance. One needed only to endure a particularly dark, unpleasant situation, just to get through to the other side of light and hope. In a juxtaposition between her father's Catholic faith and her mother's tribal heritage, she was left with an intriguing mixture of both. This too would pass.

Thus Star stood silent and motionless, enduring the feel of his arm laid heavily around her shoulders, enduring the nearness of his big bulky body next to hers, enduring the hated sound of his unctuous voice in her ears. This too would pass.

Being confronted by her stoic disposition seemed to provoke Bower into a need to provoke her. A veritable impasse of emotion, demanding more. Grinning like a loon, he reached across with his free hand to cup and lift her breast in its draping of white cotton blouse, determined to display ownership to all. Mine. This is mine.

With a hiss of outrage, she jerked free.

Her anticipated reaction neither angered nor disappointed him. Instead, pleased, his grin widened. "Ah, yes," he murmured. "I do look forward to this."

"You will look forward to your own death!" she flashed.

"Har-har-har. Someday, for sure, in bed, with a bottle of booze and a naked woman on either side of me. Raquel, kindly take the lady to her room so she can consider her—options."

The Mexican girl raised her head. Acute dislike shone from her black eyes as she said sullenly, "This way, Miss. Follow me."

The manservant, the cook, and two other retainers were allowed no chance to express their opinions, yea or nay, about this new situation. Not verbally, anyway. Certainly their expressions registered shock, dismay, doubt. Especially Horace, for whom his despicable employer could clearly sink no lower in terms of degradation and misery.

They were left to be summarily dismissed, while Star trailed along in the wake of her alleged maid.

Out of the magnificently appointed foyer, down a wide hallway laden with oil paintings, past heavy paneled doors here and there, closed against entrance. Star gave herself a mental shake. *Pay attention to what's going on, in case a chance comes along to escape!*

"In here," the maid pointed out ungraciously. "This is your room."

Cautiously Star slipped inside, glancing around the perimeter like a big cat sniffing for danger. The tone of its spaciousness, luxury, and beauty hardly registered when she was seeking out placement of windows, and their ease of opening.

"Thank you, Raquel. It is Raquel, isn't it?" At the dour nod, Star reached out with a friendly hand. "I get the sense you don't want me here."

"Why should I? He's mine, this Mr. Bower. He belongs to me. He should not have brought you here, and you should not have come."

A spasm of pity for this girl with her bruised face and unhappy eyes wrenched across Star's middle. "I wish I'd had a choice in the matter," she explained gently. "But I didn't. Believe me Raquel; I was forced into this situation. I truly do not want to be in this place."

"I don' believe you. There. The clothes he has chosen for you to wear. After you have bathed, I am to help you dress and do your hair."

Star cast a disparaging eye over the elaborate gown, spread out in rosewood, silver, and gold splendor across the bed. Everything else complete, from the high-heeled brocade shoes and sheer stockings even down to petticoats and a lacy embroidered camisole. She could easily guess at the reason for that.

"What does he think I am," she scoffed, "some sort of Spanish princess? I won't wear such a getup."

The black eyes snapped, sending furious daggers her way. "You will wear what he gives you, Miss High and Mighty, or he will punish you."

Turning from her contemplation of bolting from this velvet prison, Star felt again the wrench of pity. "As he did you?"

A shrug of dismissal. "Like he tell me, if I don' lissen, I deserve to be beat."

"Raquel!" Horrified, Star reached out once more, hoping to connect in some way. "No one deserves to be beaten. No one!"

"Maybe. Maybe not. I go fill your tub now. Then we get you ready. Mr. Bower will want to look you over before the cook puts out his evening meal."

Once she had sunk down into bubbles up to her chin, Star would admit, however namby-pamby that might make her, to thoroughly enjoying the huge tub full of water, prepared for once by hands other than her own. The rush of heat directly from a spigot, the fragrant salts and oils, the thick fluffy towel, the floor-length robe of incredible softness and warmth...such extravagance.

And to take advantage of everything Franklin Bower wished to offer, all she need do was say, "Yes." Agree to anything he desired. Adapt to his moods. Accept his foibles, his mistreatment, his twists and turns.

"No!" Belting herself into the wrapper's opulent brocade folds, Star stomped barefoot from the bathroom into the bedroom designated as hers. "No, I will not!"

Raquel glanced up, scowling, from the fabric she had been running through her fingers. "You're lucky. He never give me anything so nice as this."

"Too bad," Star spat back. "I'm sure you'd be well worth it." At what cost to her own self-respect must she try to win the allegiance and possible friendship of Bower's former bedmate?

Amazingly, the girl turned to offer a slow, calculating grin; her face, washed free of artifice and hostility, was suddenly revealed as that of a pretty, good-humored girl, caught in a web of circumstance she had neither asked for nor bargained for. "I'm sure I would be, too. You will finish getting ready now, yes?"

With a sigh, Star sank down into a padded dark wood chair near the bed. "What does he have on you, Raquel?"

"¿Perdóneme?"

"Bower. What is he using for blackmail against you? I can't really believe that you'd willingly stay in that evil man's clutches."

"I like him, Miss. I like Mr. Bower, and he—"

"Balderdash."

A shadow crossed over the girl's expression. "All right, then. I like what he can do for me. I like living in this house."

"And?"

The shadow darkened, almost into despair; only a slight whisper remained of the deep-throated voice. "He keeps my brother hostage."

"Hostage?" Star leaned forward, puzzled and curious. "How so?"

Raquel, eyes wide, visually searched the room for eavesdroppers before daring to reply, in an even softer, more confidential tone: "The silver mine, Señorita. The one Mr. Bower owns, down by the border. His men have taken slaves to work there, and one is my only brother, Benito."

"And Bower has threatened—"

"To kill him, he says, if I do not do as he say. Oh, Miss!" Tears suddenly glimmered along the girl's thick black lashes. "Please, he must not know I told you this. So many lives at stake—all those men working, under the mountain, in such terrible conditions. If I do not obey him, Mr. Bower, he will kill Benito, and everyone else!"

"And you've seen this?" Star demanded, shocked. "You know this to be true?"

"Yes, of course. A letter—I have a letter from my brother, telling me."

Star's thoughts raced to the almost equally untenable position in which her mother had been placed. There, too, a loved one's future depended solely upon another's acquiescence. Franklin Bower was a monster, trading on terror. How could he have slipped through some crack in the law for so long, without being called to account for his wrongdoings?

"There has to be something we can do," she muttered, staring off into space for several silent minutes, until, eventually, Raquel joggled her arm for attention.

"Miss, please, we have to get you dressed. And do your hair. Mr. Bower, he will be coming in soon from the ranchero, wanting his supper. Wanting you at his table. You must be ready for him, or else he might..."

Her expression grim, Star patted the girl's hand for reassurance. "All right. We'll be ready for him, don't worry. Tell me, once this meal is over, is there any way you can sneak me out of the house, help me grab a horse and run?"

Raquel backed away, mouth forming an O of opposition. "You would be a horse thief!" she hissed. "And I, too. They would hang us!"

"Only if we were caught. I need to get away, contact the authorities. We need a rescue plan, Raquel. Will you help me?"

Again that furtive scan of the room, as if the very walls were listening.

Thump! Thump!

"All right, gals, what's goin' on in there?" demanded a dreaded voice from the hallway. "I'm mighty hungry and ready t' eat. Goin' now to clean up. You gettin' dressed, Star? You helpin' her, you little Mexican hussy?"

Shivering, the maid closed her eyes and drew in a breath. "Yes, Mr. Bower, we be ready soon. I help the lady." Opening her eyes once more, her gaze met that of Star's, as she pledged, "I will help you, Miss Mendoza."

The evening meal dragged on interminably. Even in this charming hacienda, with its thick walls built of adobe and its many slanted windows, the air felt hot and stifling. Due partly to the multitude of beeswax candles lit against twilight and full dark, due also to the very heavy food that Bower seemed to prefer. How much better, in this climate, to partake of light salads and native fruits and vegetables. No, he must choose a huge beef roast to be charred over open flame and served still bloody and half-raw, and boiled potatoes with sourdough bread.

Star, seated at the foot of the expansive dining room table, opposite her host at its head, nibbled at what she could and gave up on the rest. Longing, meanwhile, for some nice fresh greens, or a cool tapioca pudding.

"How you doin' down there?" Bower wanted to know. He was sawing away at the gory mess on his plate. Occasionally this resulted in the stab of a fork, or the slosh of a spoon through some sort of broth.

"Fine."

Bower planted one elbow on the table and gestured with his knife. "Dress looks good on you, Star. Fits like a glove. Leaves bare all I wanted t' see bare."

"Yes."

She couldn't deny that the gown certainly was beautiful. Fit more for a formal banquet, possibly a castle ball, than a simple home-cooked meal, but undeniably beautiful with its range of colors and gold and silver thread. In another time, another place, she would have taken great pleasure in wearing it.

One more pause. Into his goblet he poured a second—or third—helping of wine, deep red potent wine that, held up to the light, carried all the dark mysteries of Andalusia. "That maid do all right helpin' you out and such, like I told her to?"

"Fine."

One of the staff appeared, a boy dressed in loose white tunic and pants, to bring a covered silver dish. Removing the lid, Bower leaned forward to inhale the scent of the steam with pleasure. A whisk of his hand sent the server scurrying away. "Ah. Rocky Mountain Oysters. Only it's our own brand here, native stuff right from the ranch. Want some?"

Star had gone pale. "No."

"Suit yourself." Bower was eating his way through several courses, polite enough to actually employ his napkin on occasion. "Wanna take a little walk around the place when we're finished here, get t' know each other better?"

"No."

Finished for the moment, he put down knife and fork to stare at her in the flickering candlelight. The expression in his eyes, even seen from the length of the table, sent chills chasing up and down her spine. "Not much of a talker, are you, Star?" As if that was a liability. He shrugged and reached again for the wine glass. "Don't matter. I didn't bring you here for talkin', anyway."

Her fingers tightened around each claw-foot end of the chair arms. "What, then?"

"Oh, Star, Star." Grinning, he chided her with one hand waving slowly back and forth. "I gave you credit for bein' smarter than all that. You know very damned well what I have in mind. And you came along out with me from town by your own free will."

"Under duress," she reminded him.

"You mean that little thing aboutcher maw? Hell's bells, girl, had t' convince you somehow, didn't I? And, Star..." The timbre of his voice lowered, slow and insinuating, "...you and me are gonna have us a good ole rip-roarin' time tonight, ain't we?"

Suddenly, she pushed back the weighty chair and rose, regal as a queen in her stiffened brocade and ornamental gilt. "I'm finished, thank you," she said coolly. Her manner and demeanor gave no hint of the turmoil roiling around inside or the quaking of her very bones under the fanciful gown. "I have a headache, and I'm going to my room."

"Do you now? Are you?" Frowning, he shoved upright as well, throwing down utensils with a silvery crash. "Maybe I should send the Mexican girl along, have her give you some powders or whatnot."

She inclined her head. Raquel's earlier handiwork with brush and comb had twirled her hair into an intricate knot, fastened in place by several dozen pins apparently driven straight into her skull. Costume and coiffure presented the picture of a beautiful Spanish lady, and that taken straight from any painting by one of the old masters.

"If that is your preference."

"If that is my preference. Hell, no, it's not my preference!" Kicking the chair aside, he launched himself toward her before she quite realized his intention, and seized one arm in a grip that would leave bruises. "My preference is that we head along to my bedroom, Star Mendoza," he rumbled. "You got me all lathered up, and I'm ready t' take care of business right about now."

"Mine." Star straightened, pulling herself together, gathering herself into order, ready to strike as a snake strikes—at the first opportune moment.

"What?"

"Mine. My bedroom, not yours." At least she was familiar with her own room's layout. Who knew what sort of barriers he had erected in his?

"Oh. Well, then..." A slow, lecherous smile, looking her up and down.

Bower paused, there in the dim-lit hallway, with one hand still holding her fast. The other was left free to roam, from her cheekbone still flushed by shame, to her throat, to the full breast where her heartbeat fluttered wildly, to her waist and back again. Driving her back hard against the wall, he thrust his own big quickening body up tight to hers.

A low guttural sound escaped him, brought all the way up from his midsection to explode in a great puff of breath: "Star!" as his fingers joined force to pull at her bodice and push down inside. "Star!"

"No. No, Mr. Bower," she managed to gasp.

"No?" He reared back like a rutting stallion, furious. "You dare—tell me—no—?"

"Not here. Please—not here..."

He halted long enough to glance from one side to the other. No employee would have the nerve to interrupt him in whatever he might be doing. But spying, eavesdropping? Entirely possible. She was right. Privacy was essential.

"C'mon." He seized hold of Star's upper arm, dragging her behind him. Her high-heeled shoes clattered on the wooden floor; and, contorted by the rigid control of a whalebone corset, her breath came and went in ragged spurts.

Reaching her room, Bower slammed open the door and flung her across to the bed, which she fell upon to lie, prostrate and panting, in disheveled, glorious splendor. Another halt, this time so he could survey and appreciate all the beauty that lolled helplessly there, his for the taking.

"—Been lookin' forward t' this—too long—" he muttered thickly, and kicked the door shut behind him.

Off came the boots, in a fierce, hopping-about tug of war that might have been ludicrous were it not so ominous. Then the gray pin-striped frock coat, easily enough, to be tossed aside partly inside-out; next the stock, fastened with a series of hooks and eyes that had Franklin almost howling in disgust for his manservant's help. Finally that, too, successfully undone, landed in a heap on the floor.

Stocking-footed, about to be trouser-less and shirt-less, Bower made his way to the bed.

Star was still lying half-prone, in exactly the position she had first been hurled, resting on bent elbows with skirts awry. She had uttered no more protests as to her coming fate, offered no more resistance to whatever her captor might desire.

Grinning with anticipation, he rested both fists on the mattress, one on either side to hold her prisoner, and bent forward.

Ssssttt!

In a blur of movement she had whipped free the pearl-handled Bowie knife from its sheath and slashed out. The blade caught him straight across the middle, cutting through braces, vest, and underwear, all the way down to flabby middle. Before Bower had quite realized what just happened, a thin line of blood appeared, red against the fabric. Then more blood, and pain.

"What—the hell—?"

Star had scooted backward to the headboard, arm at the ready with weapon drawn and clenched. With fear and revulsion and alarm all mixed together, the amber of her vigilant eyes had darkened to the color of molasses, and her lips had parted with an ongoing fight for breath.

Had Franklin cared to scrutinize the girl now, at this very moment, his need for immediate possession would have overridden any other desire. Franklin, however, was more concerned with the wound spurting gore from his insides than diddling someone clearly not in the mood for it.

"You—no-'count—bitch—!" he roared, stumbling toward her.

Another quick slash. This one caught him along one cheek, too near the jugular for comfort. Blood gushed forth down the front of shirt and onto the bedding.

For a moment, stunned with shock, he hesitated. Then rage took over, as red as what was pouring forth from his body in ever more increasing amounts. "God—damn—your filthy—Injun—hide—!"

Arms upraised, like a giant vulture about to strike, he reached out.

And suddenly toppled, his weight heavy and motionless upon her.

Star, shaking as if from ague, feeling half-sick with dread and despair, managed to look up.

"Hurry, Señorita!" wheezed out Raquel. In one hand she held the solid earthenware jug which she had just cracked over the back of her employer's skull. "Change, quickly, put on your old clothes, and let us be gone!"

"You—you didn't kill him—?"

"No more than you did. That one, his head is too hard and too empty to die from only a whack."

While Star struggled to free herself and her cumbersome garments from under the unconscious rancher to comply, Raquel cast one contemptuous look at the damage she had wrought.

"I'm thinkin' he will not be feelin' so good when he wakes up," she giggled. "Here, let me unhook that conquistador's dress. Then we can be on our way."

* * * * * * * * * * * * * *

"Hurry up, you damned scurvy idjuts. They got too much of a head start as it is!" Grumbling and growling like a bear fresh out of hibernation, Franklin Bower lashed his horse into greater speed.

Never mind the shortcut of rocky terrain he had decided to take. Never mind darkness lit by only a few distant stars, and none of them bright or helpful. Pursuit of the runaways was a sure thing; capture was something else again.

"Hey, boss, you're lookin' pretty bad," ventured Sykes, riding alongside. He cast a worried glance toward his employer. "Still bleedin' like a stuck pig, in fact. Hadn't you oughta sit this one out somewhere? Let us handle trackin' them two varmints."

In the pale moonlight Bower's eyes, seen under the brim of his hat, might have been those of a demon: reddened, maddened, and enraged. "Let *you* handle it?" he snarled. "When you were the ones let 'em git away? Of all the incompetent, worthless, soul-suckin' kin to vermin—!"

The rancher's head turned out to be harder than anyone, especially Raquel Garcia, had realized. While the girls had been pinning their hopes for escape on at least several hours running start, Bower had regained consciousness all too soon. Then, crawling toward the bedroom's doorway, he had bawled for help.

Shocked to the core of his aristocratic being, Horace had assembled medical supplies and begun attending to a multitude of wounds. Something like this would certainly never take place in his part of the world. The very idea!

Shortly, with bandages wrapped tightly around the gaping slit in his middle, sticking plaster applied to the slice on his cheek, and a thorough if hasty washing and rinsing done of the head wound, Bower was able to change into ranch gear. Urged to rest and recover by even those who disliked him, such as his manservant, Franklin let his fury carry him along.

"Goddamn whores," he raged, swigging from the nearest bottle of rum. Enough spirits might dull the worst of his pain; enough would also fuel the fire until this night was over and he'd done what he was setting out to do. "Stole my best horse, did they? I could string 'em up. I could send 'em to hell in a hand basket. Sweet Jesus, this hurts! Goddamn fancy-dressed fancy-talkin' sluts!"

No one had noticed the disappearance; no one had heard any sound of departure.

"Goddamn blind fools. I should fire the lot of you!" fumed Bower.

Physically impaired, and with a brain not exactly clicking along as it should be, still, while forced to sit quietly for his manservant's medical care, he was already working out a plan. He was done with both these jezebels. Who needed all this aggravation, when there were plenty of other fish in the sea? No. They would be recaptured and returned to the Condor Ranch.

Then...well, what came next would not be pleasant.

Bandaged, changed, well-lit by alcohol and a giant smelly cigar, Bower had gathered his men together to explain their mission. "First off, Felipe, I need you to get hold of Suarez. Tell him all hell'sa poppin' and I need him here at the ranch. Pronto. The resta you boys, saddle up. There's a job t' get done, and it's time you earn your pay. Move out!"

* * * * * * * * * * * *

The weight of either girl, singly, would hardly cause a strain for any horse. Taken together, however, after a while even the strongest mount would begin to tire. As this one was doing now.

"How much farther do you think it is to town?" whispered Star.

Sound carried a long distance, up here in the hills. Best to be as quiet as possible.

"Hard to tell," said Raquel, peering through trees and brush. A few minutes ago she had slid to the ground to reconnoiter, because they had apparently wandered into unfamiliar territory. "A back road, like this—not sure of miles. Or time."

Silence for a few minutes. She led the stallion forward, around a mound of boulders, down a small knoll. A softened, quiet path, filled with powdery dust, some pine needles, dead leaves. So little light, such a huge space.

"I'm sorry for what you've gone through at Franklin Bower's filthy hands," Star offered. "He's a horrible man, and we need to bring charges against him. We need to rescue all the people he's hurt."

A sliver of moon shone in the sky. Raquel turned, glancing up over her shoulder. "Bring charges how?" she scoffed. "Who would believe us, you and me? Him a white man, with all the rights in the world; he'd be laughin' when they put us both in jail."

The unfairness of it, pitting one race against the other: that's what had held her back from reporting Bower's past offenses. And now... "I know. I understand. And I'm worried, too, about my mother, about what may come up to haunt her."

"Your mother. My brother. He holds all the cards," said Raquel bitterly. "And we pay the price."

"Maybe not. I have a good friend in the sheriff of San Francisco. And—and another...lawman, possibly..."

"Here. We are through the rough part. I think I know now where we are." The girl approached, grabbed hold of the reins, and swung herself onto the horse, behind her companion. "One sheriff, good. But, Señorita, I think maybe not the whole town. Move on, Cyclone."

An easy trot took them from the forested hills to an open road, flat and smooth and accessible. Traitorously so. In that space the half-dozen Condor riders unexpectedly emerged, thundering along from out of nowhere to overtake and surround.

Even vastly outnumbered, they fought, until there was no fight left in either of them. Pulled kicking and screaming from their horse, the girls were dragged before judge and jury, Franklin Bower. He sat wavering in his saddle, worn and shadowed like some bloodthirsty demon from the depths of hell.

"I hoped you were dead!" Star spat out at him.

He stared down at her, implacable, immovable. At the veil of black hair torn loose from its braid, at the lovely face registering open contempt, at the body held tight and fettered that he had planned to possess. "No such luck, Miss Mendoza," he said tonelessly. Then, to the two men securing her position, he ordered. "Hit her. Now."

Open-mouthed, they gawked at each other. "Hit her? Hit a woman? But—Mr. Bower, you can't—"

"Do you see this?" he thundered, gesturing to the bandages still oozing gore. "Do you see what she did to me? B'sides, she ain't nothin' but a half-breed. Hit her, I said!"

Still hesitation. Then the slow scrape of a pistol being drawn from its holster, and the cold cock of a trigger being pulled back. Bower, obviously nearly ready to collapse, leaned forward onto the saddle horn to brace himself.

"If I was able to, I'd be down there, beatin' her ass. So I have t' leave it up t' you. Which is it gonna be, boys? Her? Or you?"

Anyone confronted by a weapon held ready to fire knows that the only option available is surrender.

Sykes' open-handed slap came before she was ready to bear it. Hard. Fast. Vicious. Flung sideways by the force of the blow, Star let out a cry. Then came the second. With it, and another louder cry, she crumpled helplessly in the dust.

"Is she bleedin'? Good. Just a little payback, trollop. As for you—" His attention turned toward Raquel, quailing between her captors, "—I can't blame you quite as much. You're too damned stupid to see how she was just suckin' you up into her schemes. Still... Oh, hell, smack her around a little, too, fellahs. Show her how you don't screw over the big boss."

Several punches, some kicks, and numerous screams and tears later, Bower surveyed the scene before him. Master of his domain, and of a great deal of northern California. Against the pain in his midriff, he managed a rusty chuckle. "Didn't really think you'd get away from me, didja? Dunderheads."

Both women had been dragged to their feet, bruised and battered, weaving a little, and unsteady, standing upright only because their captors supplied support.

From the height of his stallion, Bower looked them over. "I'm done with the both of you. We get back to the Condor, it's farewell and adios, ladies. Oh, no—" at Star's unintentional flinch, "I ain't gonna kill you. Not even a half-breed pup like you, Miss Snooty-Pants Mendoza. Naw. I got a better plan. You ever heard of Suarez?"

With a gasp of horror, Raquel tried to pull free. "Señor, please—no! Oh, please, for the love of God...I will do anything, anything—!"

"Oh, yeah, sweet little girl, I just bet you will. And, y'know, you bein' so willin', and all, I may just change my mind, keep you around on the ranch, after all. Maybe it'll just be Star here that gets taken away." Pleased, Bower chuckled again and included his employees in the explanation. "'Case you don't know the name, boys, Suarez runs a band of banditos hereabouts."

"Suarez?" repeated Russell Sykes, incredulous. "You're dealin' with the likes of him?"

"Yessir, I am. Got himself involved in the sex trade, too. Good money in it, and don't we know. Word is he's mighty hard on his women, but—" the very slightest of shrugs, with care for the bandaged wound, "this curvy ol' catamount should get herself trained right well."

"But—Suarez?" Clearly Sykes was having some trouble with the notion.

"That's what I said!" snapped Bower. "Now mount up. Let's head on home so I can get the rest of this business taken care of."

Chapter 8

By the next morning, with no word from or mention of Star anywhere in town, Frances Goddard was becoming more and more alarmed. At the breakfast table, over slices of ham and new-laid scrambled eggs, she tackled her brother.

"Well, yeah, I agree it does seem strange we haven't seen hide nor hair of her for two days now," agreed William, comfortably sipping at his coffee. Much better tasting than the foul brew he seemed to come up with at the sheriff's office...even if he wouldn't admit that to anyone. How exactly did his sister put things together to fix something so darned good? Maybe if he washed out the pot a little more often than—oh, say, once a month or so... "What?"

"If you would pay attention to the subject at hand, Will," said Frances with forced patience, "I said: it isn't just me wondering where she's gotten to. Several others asked me yesterday if she's gone out of town. And I don't think she has. Not without telling *me*, anyway. Why, I'm the closest friend she's got in these parts."

A bite of juicy ham, perfectly cooked; another forkful of fluffy eggs: delicious. Will wondered if Sarah Coleman liked to cook, and whether she was handy in the kitchen. It paid to know these things in advance.

"William! Stop woolgathering and listen to me!"

He squinted up at her, standing across from him with hands on hips in her favorite confrontational position. "I am listenin', Frannie. I know you're worried. And I'm startin' to feel that way a mite, myself. Tell you what. Soon's I finish, let's go check out her cabin again, see if she's there. And if she ain't--"

"Sheriff! Hey, Sheriff! Will!" A pounding at the front door, and shouting to beat the band.

"Lands sake, what on earth is going on?"

But Frances didn't get a chance to stomp through the hall in answer to the summons, because William beat her to the punch. He had already picked up his Stetson and was gone before she could even put aside the fry pan.

An exchange of voices from the porch: one she recognized as Clement's, his deputy, raised and excited; the other was William's, calm and easy-going as always, just the sort of response San Francisco's citizenry appreciated in a crisis situation. Apparently this was.

"Hey, Frannie." William poked his head around the corner. "Got us a good ol' riot down by some saloon on the wharf. Feller come off a ship with what people are claimin' might be some kinda plague, and the whole place is up in arms. I gotta go down there now, with Clem, maybe deputize me a few men."

"But, Will—" Troubled by the problematic start to what had dawned as a golden day, she trailed into the foyer for further discussion.

He was already fastening on his badge and gun belt, taking on the woes of world, focusing on what must be done to restore order. Yet a small kernel of his busy thoughts remained centered on her worries about Star.

"Now, don'cha fret, honey. I'll send somebody to ferret out Matt Yancey and he can go with you. You wait for him, y'hear? Don't want you hightailin' it off on your own—never know what you might run into. And best if you got yourself an experienced lawman along, in any case. Got it?"

Warm relief flooded her veins. As often as she chided or teased her brother, he was a dear, devoted individual, and she loved him for it. "Got it. Thank you, Will."

"Not sure when I'll be home, Frannie. Might be a long day."

And possibly a dangerous one. By comparison, her concerns suddenly seemed minor. Reaching up, she flung her arms around his neck and kissed him soundly on the cheek. "Be careful, William. Please be careful."

* * * * * * * * * * * * * *

"You comfy cozy in there, Miss Goddard?"

"I'm just fine, Matt, thank you. Please, call me Frances, for heaven's sake. And please, please, can we be on our way now? So much wasted time..." She was all but wringing her hands with anxiety.

As promised, Matt Yancey had shown up shortly after William's abrupt departure. With the brief explanation that wasn't really an explanation, he had taken it upon himself to move forward, hitching up the Goddard buggy to their rather overweight mare and helping Frances into the seat.

"Good t' see you're wearin' somethin' sensible," he approved, flicking the reins.

She glanced down at her prim white blouse, pleated navy skirt, and low-heeled black boots. "Oh. Plain and unadorned, you mean?"

Matt grinned. "No, ma'am, you ain't catchin' me in that trap. What I meant was—no consarned giant hoops to get in the way."

"I see. Well, you'll be relieved to know that I rarely wear those consarned giant hoops. They're a nuisance, especially if the wind hits you just right. So, tell me," in a patent effort to shift her apprehensive thoughts, "what is young Rob up to today?"

Pushing back his hat, so that the hair curled and corkscrewed into ringlets to frame his face, he related the latest doings of Master Robert. "We've been spendin' a lotta time together, doin' this and that. He was a mite disappointed not t' be comin' along today, but Sarah's workin' on laundry and says she can use his help. That'll keep the boy outa mischief."

Riding in a carriage might not provide as much physical exercise as a good brisk walk, but it was certainly a speedier method of transport. Within just a few minutes they had arrived at Star's cabin, still sleeping under the summer sun.

"No changes, from what I see," observed Frances doubtfully. "And no damage."

Springing easily to the ground, Matt moved to assist his passenger and they started toward the front door. California poppies the color of an ocean sunset swayed gently in a breeze, as did a pair of calico curtains at one open window.

"And still unlocked." Carefully he pushed at the handle. Nothing untoward, as yet. A quick, cursory glance around inside, then another quick glance at the shed. Ezekiel, lonesome for some company, brayed a greeting.

"It's the strangest thing," Frances murmured. "How could Star have simply disappeared like that?"

The circuits had begun to connect in her razor-sharp brain while she considered the situation; and Matt, who had seen this sort of thing before, stood patiently by and waited, letting the world pass him by. Leaning against the fence rail, he crossed one ankle over the other and gave the mule a few friendly pats.

Bees zoomed here and there, gathering pollen from a garden of colorful flowers; butterflies, too, but taking a more leisurely, more graceful flight. Overhead a hawk slowly circled, searching for prey. White puffs of cloud gathered, formed, and drifted past.

"Do you have other matters awaiting your attention today, Matt?" she asked suddenly.

"No, ma'am. Nothin' more important than tendin' to whatever you'd like me to do."

Frances smiled. "Oh, you are one very nice, dependable man. Very well, then. Here's the plan. We must go call on Star's parents."

"Her parents? Thought they were out in the wild somewhere, hard to find?"

"Only," said Frances smugly, "if you don't know where to look. And I know exactly. Remember, Star was my pupil for a number of years. During that time I was pleased to conduct occasional home visits, talk with the families, nip any potential problems in the bud—that sort of thing. Yes, indeed, Matt. I know exactly where to look."

And thus the journey resumed, to a much more far-flung place than Matt had envisioned.

For some time, the buggy wheels hummed along on what passed for a paved road, fairly smooth, packed-down dirt, with large rocks and larger boulders pushed off the side. All too soon, however, the convenience of that road ended, fading away into mere wagon tracks cut into the desert expanse—through pungent sagebrush and clumps of deergrass, woodbalm and milkweed and dwarf coyote bush, flowering pink bush mallow and creeping green yerba buena.

"That was its original name, you know," Frances, squinting into the distance, offered suddenly.

"Huh?"

"The city of San Francisco. Literally, good herb. An aromatic mint."

He glanced her way with a slow smile, whose effect Frances could feel from her toes to her susceptible heart. *Oh, Star, could you have seen that very same smile and deliberately shut down your own reaction to it?*

"Just makin' conversation, are you?" asked the owner of that devastating smile.

"Just giving you some local history," Frances replied, a trifle crossly. "It's always helpful to be familiar with an area you've just come into, don't you think?"

"Like this damned desert that ain't got a soul in sight, maybe. You sure you know the way? You sure you come out here before in a buggy, 'stead of on hawseback?"

Frances sniffed. "You're following the trail, aren't you? Star makes this trip every few weeks, with her cart and her mule. Have a little faith, Matthew."

"Faith t' take a trail fulla bumps and ruts? Sure a lotta jouncin' here. I'd be surprised if we don't both end up bruised from top to bottom."

"Surely you're used to this sort of thing," she said, surprised, "from your traveling around with the Rangers."

"Yes and no. Didn't drive no wagon over the buffalo wallers, I rode my own good stallion. Lissen, y' think we're anywheres near this place yet, or have we landed on the far side of the moon?"

"So glad you have a sense of humor. That's important in a man."

"In a woman, too. Makes rubbin' along in life together a lot easier. Well?"

"There."

"There where?"

"That Manzanita grove, farther off, closer to that small mountain." Frances pointed. "See it? And that's a good sign—smoke from a fire. So someone is home. Let's hope it's Star."

She was not alone in that hope.

What little time Matt had spent with the girl, two days ago, had left him wanting more. He, too, felt anxious and apprehensive as to Star's whereabouts. And her safety. However self-reliant and independent she might be, some situations could turn out to be just too problematic, too formidable, for one of the fair sex to deal with. Especially one so young and lovely...and, he would admit it, quite desirable.

"Adsila!" Too worked up to wait for assistance, Frances clambered down from the buggy's high seat, skirts awhirl, and started across the open ground. "Adsila, are you here?"

"Frances!" hissed Matt, who was busy tying the mare in a shady spot. "Wait a darned minute. You dunno—"

"Of course I do. Look."

From the open door of a small cabin, very similar in style and form to Star's own, emerged a woman dressed in simple doeskin— dress, leggings, and moccasins. Very little of the fancy beadwork so often seen on such apparel, for this would be, like the clothing of her Yankee sisters, more of a work uniform. Clearly, Adsila had been working.

Or perhaps not. She was approaching like a runaway train, careening down the small knoll toward them while making some sort of keening noise, loud and long.

My God. Horrified, Matt was drawn up short. *That sounded like a mourning cry. What would come next, the braids chopped off and fire ash rubbed into the skin?*

"Adsila, what is it?" Frances met the Cherokee woman halfway, taking her right into the sanctuary of her open arms. "What's wrong?"

"Miss Goddard. Miss Goddard. It is my Goldenstar...please, you must help me!" Plaintive sobs that would tear at the fabric of anyone's heart.

"Has she been hurt, Adsila? Please tell us, what can we do?"

Shorter by several inches, she looked tearfully up at the teacher who had been friend to her family for many years. "Not out here. You will come into my house, yes? And let me explain?"

Over her shoulder, across the small intervening distance, Frances exchanged a meaningful glance with her escort. "I think that would be a good idea. If it's all right with you, we'll both come inside," she said firmly.

The large main room held a living area, with hand-made wooden furniture and hand-loomed multicolored blankets, a stone fireplace almost big enough to roast a buffalo, a Spartan kitchen dominated by table and chairs. There, gestured Adsila, would her guests please take a seat and be comfortable. While she poured coffee into enamelware mugs, Frances carried out introductions.

"And you are a lawman, Mr. Yancey?" their hostess confirmed, still shaky but regaining purpose. Upset though she was, it was plain to see where Star had gotten her looks. This was a beautiful woman by any measurement. "Good. We have not much time."

"Star is missing," Frances guessed.

"Missing? She has been taken!" Another surge of tears, and a half-sob, quickly bitten back. "My girl—my precious girl—in the hands of that—that *bastardo!*"

"Um." Frances sent a wincing sort of glance Matt's way. "A—um—Spanish word..."

"Yeah," said Matt grimly. "I get the meanin'. Go on, please."

If suntanned Cherokee skin could ever be blanched by emotion, certainly Adsila's was today. How many hours had she spent fretting and fussing, helpless out here in the middle of nowhere?

"I blame him—Daniel's brother, Ricardo. He is the one mixed up with that gang. And yet—and yet—" Drawing in a ragged breath, she pressed her knuckles tight to her lips, as if the physical discomfort could alleviate some of the emotional pain building up and about to explode. "Had he not been there, had he not let me know—*eee*—!"

"Adsila." Frances' stern voice pulled her friend back to reality. "Daniel's brother? A gang? But where is Daniel?"

The mental battle to explain as clearly and succinctly as possible could be discerned as the woman straightened her slender shoulders and lifted her chin. "Two days past, he left. Checking his trap lines, as he always does. So he is not here. He does not know his only child is—"

"Is where, Mrs. Mendoza?" Matt interrupted the labored recital. "Where is Star?"

"Captive—captive of that monster, Suarez!"

Frances gasped. "Oh, dear God!" she whispered.

"Suarez," repeated the Ranger, looking from one to the other. "Who's Suarez? And where would he be right now?"

"Suarez is a bandito. Leader of a Mexican gang. A terrible gang, Matt. They're murderers, every one of them, and thieves, and they supply drugs and liquor, and they—" Deeply distressed, Frances lowered her voice, as if a softer tone might negate actual fact. "—they purchase—women, Matt. They're slave traders. If Star has been kidnapped by—by that bunch of thugs—"

His expression has suddenly been set into a mask, hard and still as granite. "Yeah, Frances. Kinda got an idea of what they'll do to her. You say your husband's brother told you Star had been taken captive, Mrs. Mendoza?"

More tears rimmed the thick dark lashes, and then overflowed. Adsila nodded.

"And this is his niece? His own goddamned niece? Jesus Christ on a handcart!" Matt swore in disbelief. Unable to contain himself any longer, he heaved to his feet with a great scraping and scuffing of the chair and began to pace.

"Did Ricardo tell you when this happened?" asked Frances gently.

"Yesterday—late yesterday morning she was seen being driven out of town by Franklin Bower."

"Franklin Bower!" Aghast, Frances gulped down some hot coffee, holding the cup with unsteady hands. "So he's mixed up in this, too."

"She tried to get away, last night," continued the girl's mother, disconsolate. "But Mr. Bower followed and—and he brought her back to his ranch. This morning—Ricardo told me that this morning my Star was sold—sold!—to Suarez!" This was finished on a wail, as Adsila buried her face in both hands to weep bitterly and convulsively.

Matt returned to the table for his own gulp of coffee. And then another. In an aside, he realized how savory this brew was. Given a contest between Adsila's and William's, her concoction would win, hands down.

"That explains why she wasn't at the cabin when I went lookin' for her," he mused. "But why would she have gone with Bower, after all her problems with him in the past? Why would she even consider just calmly drivin' away beside him, in his carriage?"

Adsila looked up, features white as paste. "I think because she was protecting me."

Pulling out the chair he had shoved away, Matt straddled its seat and crossed his arms along its back. "I know we're pressed for time here, and we gotta get goin' soon. But first I have to have all the facts or I'm no good t' anybody. So tell me, Mrs. Mendoza, please. What was she protectin' you from?"

Those dark eyes had seen so much pain and misunderstanding, from childhood on. She sighed a deep, long-suffering sigh that came straight from the heart and a lifetime of memories. "An attempted murder charge," she whispered.

"Adsila!"

"Yes, my friend?" The weary, reddened eyes shifted. "You will no longer want to be my friend, when you hear my story."

Frances reached across the table to clasp hands and grip tight. "There's nothing you can tell me that would change our friendship," she said fiercely. "Now go on, let us hear what happened. And quickly."

"I was only sixteen when I came to Yerba Buena for the first time," Adsila, staring down at the bleached table top before her, began softly. "It was also the last."

Her mother was far too shy to face a strange tribe of people with brown or white faces and unknown ways; her father, who had broken his ankle in a fall and was still recovering, could not accompany her. Instead, she was escorted by two of her cousins, Bitterroot, neither as pretty nor as vivacious but quite responsible, and the proud and stalwart warrior, Tamarack.

Trading with a Mexican owner of the general store had been accomplished easily and to the satisfaction of both parties: furs and pottery and other handmade items in exchange for ammunition,

Yanqui blankets, a few items of clothing, and various other sundries. The owner's son, a handsome black-eyed young man named Daniel, had helped carry their purchases to the wagon parked and waiting. Things seemed to be going well, in this burgeoning little settlement by the bay.

And then Tamarack had discovered firewater.

Several white men, turning a covetous eye toward two fair young Indian maidens, decided it would be necessary—and probably amusing, besides—to sidetrack the watchful young Indian brave. What better way than camaraderie, and a saloon?

It didn't take long, for someone completely unused to the taste and effect of hard spirits. Within a short time, Tamarack was stewed to the gills, staggering along from place to place, and riotously funny for anyone watching.

Then the watchers could tackle the girls.

That took place in the dusk of early evening, in an alley near the storefront which Tamarack had entered, for some unknown reason. Still befuddled, he emerged just as they were being dragged away, fighting off their assailants and screaming for help. Their cries reached him, through the fog; it was his duty to protect and guard, was it not? Pulling his knife from its sheath, he had stumbled to the rescue.

"Two of the men were stabbed," said Adsila quietly, recounting the sorrowful memories.

"One very badly; he seemed to be dying. Bitterroot had been—she had been hurt in the attack."

"Oh, my dear," Frances whispered in utmost sympathy. "What a terrible experience."

"The three of us were able to reach the wagon, ready to leave. But the last man gave chase, shouting that we—we were all thieves, and murderers. He grabbed me, pulling me away, just as Tamarack and Bitterroot made their escape. From what I later heard, they arrived safely at our village, with no further—adversity..."

"And you?" asked Matt. "What happened t' you?"

She looked up with the barest hint of a smile. It warmed her face into rare beauty, like sunlight breaking through the clouds after a rainstorm. "That nice young man, Daniel Mendoza, raced out to save me. He and his family kept me with them, until the ruckus had died down. Eventually, as you know..."

"You and Daniel were married and moved out here, away from the scandal." Frances nodded. "That explains so much, Adsila."

Matt, head bent, had been closely following the story, listening to every detail. Now he said, "I'm sorry for makin' you go through all this again, Mrs. Mendoza. But I don't quite understand why you'd be the one worryin' about attempted murder. You said your cousin, this Tamarack—"

"I said he pulled his knife. I was the one who used it."

A gasp of pure shock from Frances.

Adsila turned her way. "Yes. You see, now. You understand."

"He was too drunk to function? Ahuh. And where is he at the moment?"

"Dead. Of too much drink, over the years."

The muscles around Matt's mouth tightened. After another sip of the cooling coffee, he asked, "And the other girl—Bitterroot?"

"Also dead. Of shame. She hanged herself next day, from the tallest oak in our village."

"Oh, dear Lord. Oh, Adsila..." Frances' eyes had filled with sympathetic moisture. And Frances did not cry easily. But surely such a story of unmitigated tragedy merited the tribute of a few tears.

The Ranger was not quite finished. "Is this common knowledge? No? Then how did Bower find out about it?"

Adsila lifted one shoulder in a very un-Cherokee-like shrug. "His brother was the one most badly wounded."

"Son of a bitch," muttered Matt. An understatement, if ever there was one.

Frances murmured something about this being beyond her, slid away from the table, and strode over to the open door. So much had filled this morning's hours already, and yet the sun was only directly overhead. In the shade of a Manzanita, her plump mare dozed, occasionally swished her tail at a persistent fly, and dozed again.

"And you're sure you've been charged with attempted murder?" she asked from the threshold.

"So Mr. Bower has been quick to tell me, every time he's come here."

"Ah. That's interestin'."

Concealing a crime, harassing a victim, serving as accessory—Franklin Bower might have a lot to answer for in court.

Matt rose, reached out to lightly touch the back of Adsila's hand, resting on the table, and picked up his hat. "Mrs. Mendoza, thank you for bein' so cooperative. I know this whole thing has been hangin' over your head for a long while, and it's about time we get it cleared up."

"You'll help her with that, Matthew?"

"I will, for sure. And so will Sheriff Goddard. Now, tell me where this Suarez individual and his camp might be found. We gotta get a-skally-hootin'."

* * * * * * * * * * * * * * * *

"Goddamnit, I knew we shoulda ridden out here by our own selves," grumbled Matt, impatiently flicking the reins at the mare's ladylike backside. "When you're in a hurry, you don't wanna sit in a goddamned buggy behind a goddamned fat hawse who's takin' her sweet time t' move along. Can't this nag go any faster?"

"Here, Matt, let me handle her. She's used to my voice. Hi, there, Veronica. Come on, girl, geeup!"

"Veronica! What the hell kinda dumbass name is that?"

"Matthew Yancey." Glaring at him as if he were a reprehensible student in her school, sowing wild oats, she said severely, "You stop that cursing right this very minute. Veronica is a fine name, and she's a fine horse. Just sit there silently and fume if you must. But don't take out your bad mood on us."

He fumed for only a minute or two. Then, dredging up a more deferential expression, he apologized for his bad behavior.

"It's all right, Matt. I understand. We're both worried, and anxious to find that girl." Frances peered sideways. "What do you think our chances are?"

"I think it's a helluva mess," he replied gloomily, staring off at the horizon. "Wanna know the truth? Our odds—they ain't s' very good."

That kept her quiet for the rest of the journey back to town. Quiet, ruminating, and distressed.

At the Yancey household, reached in early afternoon, Matt swung down from the buggy, with the assurance from Frances that of course she could return to her own home and unhitch the tired mare by herself, she'd been doing it for years. And, yes, she promised that she would track down William, by hook or by crook, describe the day's adventures in detail, and relay the message urging a desperate need for help.

"He's gotta follow me down to *Los Huesos*, Frannie," Matt paused only to give last-minute instructions. "Tell him t' take the Glen Creek Road south. And t' bring as many men as he can find, and as much ammo as he can put together. Lord knows what we'll find there."

"I will, Matt," Frances assured him. She rested one hand upon the width of his brawny shoulder, as a pledge. "Be careful."

"Yes, ma'am." A brief salute of his hat, and he wheeled away.

* * * * * * * * * * * * * *

Los Huesos, Matt snorted as they thundered along. *The Bones.* Another helluva dumbass name. Did the people in this barmy state lack imagination? And just what was he heading for, anyway—some kind of ancient kids' game or a burial site?

Good thing he hadn't taken Colonel out to the Mendoza place today after all. Lazing around the shady corral till now meant that his big black steed was fresh and ready for this afternoon's crucial ride.

Sarah had reacted to his news about the visit to see Star's mother with her usual cool competence. Of course she could manage the household, and his son, while Matt was off fighting desperadoes. And while she was at it, here: take this along, and this, and he might need that…

Now, both he and his horse were loaded down. Gun belt refilled and rifle in its scabbard, with plenty of extra ammunition for both; bedroll and slicker tied behind the saddle; canteen of fresh water, hunks of beef jerky and a dozen buttermilk biscuits stuffed into a drawstring cotton bag; jacket, gloves, extra shirt and socks; piggin' string rope, lariat, and fresh-sharpened hunting knife; war bag and scarf—all the paraphernalia of the trail he had thought not to use again for a long time. At least, not until his return to the Rangers.

Following the directions given to Adsila Mendoza by her brother-in-law—*and what a family relationship that must be!*—Matt had kept his stallion at a steady gallop for some time along the meanderings of Glen Creek. Then a brief break, a rest for both, then another steady gallop.

Stay the course. Don't rush your fences. Keep it true and sure. Remember that fable of the tortoise and the hare.

While he pressed forward, hunkered down against his own disquieting reflections about Star, and what terrible harm might have already been inflicted upon her, the scenery passed by unnoticed. Forests of giant madrones, tall and spreading full with summer's leafage; grassland and shrubbery galore; the Creek itself, narrow enough and shallow enough to wade across, pinned in place by boulders and pine.

If Matt were a spiritual man, he'd be praying a blue streak about now. *God, let her be safe. God, keep her goin' until I get there. God, help her survive whatever might be happenin'. God, give me guts to kill anyone who's hurt her.*

The smoke from a cooking fire not far in the distance gave unexpected but welcome warning of habitation. The Suarez gang, and his hideout of *Los Huesos,* parked back in hills where no one else would think to look?

"Whoa, Colonel, let's slow down a bit, boy," he murmured, pulling back on the reins. With that, and several good affectionate pats on the muscular neck, obedience was immediate, from a hard gallop to a trot to a slow walk, hoof beats muffled by the powdery dust underfoot.

Curbed to a full stop, but still willing to run with the wind, Colonel fought his bit just a little. Then submission, and a soft whicker.

"Yeah, I know, fellah." Matt swung down and dropped the reins. Prepared thus, the stallion would stand until gathered up for action once more. "Gotta take a look around. Hang on, I'll be back."

The afternoon was waning, with soft golden light filtering through the trees, turning all it touched to a Midas glow. From rough worn boulder to bushy mesquite to solid trunk of live oak to furry green cypress, Matt moved quickly and stealthily, with hunting knife drawn and Colt at the ready. His boots made no sound, serving only to kick up little puffs of soft dirt with every step.

Noise reached him: the occasional sound of male laughter, raucous and scornful; several voices here and there, conversing in low-toned Spanish, issuing forth taunts or threats or filthy banter; a horse's whinny, hastily subdued, then another. He was near enough now to see someone dumping an armful of broken branches onto the fire, sending up sparks. Why not? The area was suitably secluded to prevent discovery, far from civilization, tucked into hills where no one would reasonably go exploring, except for a reason.

Matt had a reason.

Squinting against the golden light, so deceptively pleasing, so deceptively obscuring, he cast about this *Los Huesos* camp, taking careful note of the number of outlaws, their location scattered throughout, and their function.

Several were engaged in some sort of gambling game, with ivory-colored pieces. Ah. That must be the bones. A couple more lay sound asleep atop gaily striped blankets, propped against their saddles, snoring lustily. Another was lounging near the fire, drinking from a bottle of tequila and barking an occasional order. *El Jefe*, Suarez himself?

Damn. Probably a dozen of the nesting cobras, if not more.

"¿Dónde está la puta?" the drinker wanted to know at one point, while Matt crouched watching and waiting.

"¡Está aquí!" came a response from across the camp. "Es muuuuy bonita," the bandito finished up, in oily tones of great delight that drew appreciative hoots and hollers from the gamesmen. "We use her pronto, ¿es verdad?"

Small need to pinpoint that voice, because its owner had retreated in the opposite direction from the main camp. Clearly, a guard. Or separated for privacy while he did whatever he planned on doing?

Matt silently counted to ten, banishing the blinding red mist of fury, calming his nerves. Only cool, rational action would win the day and rescue Star from these dangerous hooligans.

He couldn't help wondering, rather wistfully, if William and a posse of armed, trusted lawmen might even now be on the way.

A movement some feet away; Señor Hot to Trot, whistling some hat dance tune, was wandering away from wherever he had Star confined, off to a grove of shrubbery beyond. And, still whistling, was unbuttoning his trousers as he went.

Ha. A piss in the woods would keep him occupied while Matt sneaked around from the other side. Easily done. And with deep, abiding pleasure.

Thunk!

The butt of Matt's revolver whacked across the back of *el bandito's* skull sent him face downward onto a patch of dead pine needles, without even the hint of a groan. Holstering the Colt, he kept firm hold of his Bowie as he duck-walked backward, in retreat. Returned to his original position, he scanned the area once again.

There she was. Star, trussed up like a Christmastime goose, gagged, wrists bound together, ankles bound together, flung on the ground in a heap of old clothes and misery. A badly bruised face, as far as he could tell: swollen and battered and bloodied from temple to throat; white blouse spattered by dirt and gore, torn apart, gaping free over warm café au lait flesh.

He emerged from cover. No one else in sight yet. *Hurry, hurry; but don't make a hash of it!*

Her eyes widened in shock and disbelief when she spied him scurrying closer. Then they closed, as if this nightmare had merely produced another illusion, and a tear slipped free to ooze down her cheek.

At the first sense of a knife slicing through her bonds, Star came to life. First the ankles, then the wrists, and the hated ropes were gone.

Matt touched her shoulder in warning, even as he pulled the gag from between her teeth, and silenced her slightest sound with a finger to his lips.

Her limbs had gone numb from lack of circulation. As he helped her upright, she nearly collapsed with the pain of new blood flowing through her veins. Halting, limping, half-carrying, half-crawling, somehow he got her away from the camp and her captors and off into the woods. There Colonel waited, steady and dependable.

At last, Matt could steal one precious minute to sweep her into his embrace. "Star," he breathed over the rapid thud of his heartbeat. "Oh, my God. Star!"

"You came," she whispered, still dazed by her unexpected rescue. "You came for me. Thank you, Matt…Oh, how I—thank you—" and ended there, choking on relief.

Easily he swung her onto the back of his horse, then climbed into the saddle. "Hang on," he gave warning. "Gotta fly, Star. Hang on tight."

Chapter 9

"Damn. Damn it to hell. Shoulda killed the bastard."

"What is it, Matt?" Star spoke his name as if she couldn't repeat it often enough. A woman thoroughly used to and at home in the out-of-doors, she had wrapped her arms around his waist, leaned her poor abraded face against the bracing width of his shoulder blades, and let her heels dangle loose along the stallion's loins. "Is there a problem?"

"You might say so." His voice held a disgusted tone. Not worried. Not yet. His acute sense of hearing had caught the sounds behind them; faint, so far, and distant, but approaching. "The fellah I clomped over the head musta come to a lot sooner than I figured, and he raised the alarm. We got company followin' us."

Along the whole length of his spine, warmed by the press of her lavish breasts crushed tight and close, he could feel her stiffen with foreboding. "Will they catch us? Matt, if they catch us—if they catch us—" a hitch of breath like a hiccup, "—I won't survive their taking me a second time."

He reached down one hand to cover both of hers, clasped together over his midriff. "It won't happen, Star," he pledged. "I won't let it happen."

She wanted to believe him. She longed to believe him. But his horse was carrying double, at a solid, tooth-jarring gallop, and the outlaw gang behind them were riding fresh mounts.

Soon it wasn't only the pounding of hoof beats they heard, but jeers and shouts. Closer. Coming closer. Then it was a gunshot. Somewhere off in the distance, the bullet smacked into an ancient tree with stunning force. Another gunshot, still by a wide miss. The rifle shot that whizzed by next was not so wide.

Shivering, Star jounced along like a bag of used laundry, shrunk down and hung onto Matt for dear life. Now he was urging the stallion to greater speed, swinging first to the left, then to the right and back again. No reason to provide an easy target, especially when that target was the girl locked in a death-grip behind him.

"M-M-M-Matt," she chattered. "Too near. They're getting too near."

"I know. I know, Star. Doin' my best."

His fingers tightened over hers. Much as she had hoped being next to his big sturdy body would offer reassurance, it wasn't working. She was terrified. Being thrown willy-nilly into the clutches of depravation, with no hope of escape or rescue, had shown her a great dearth of spirit, the true depths of fear. She had never before known such nerve-jangling, gut-twisting, blood-freezing terror.

"Matt."

"Yeah, Star."

"Matt, if they catch us—" she gulped, "—if they catch us, I want you to promise me something."

"Anything."

"That you will kill me."

This time it was he who shivered. "For God's sake, Star—"

"I mean it, Matt. You don't know what—what they planned to do, what they—what they planned to have me do! Oh, Matt!" she cried, frantic, "promise, if we don't make it out, that you will do this thing for me!"

"Goldenstar," he said between his teeth; over the racketing of the horse his voice was barely audible. "We'll make it out. That much I promise."

They were in the open now, being carried across a width and length of tangled meadow grass that stretched from horizon to horizon under the lowering sun. Matt had bent low over his saddle, like a jockey, as if to urge the stallion onward, and Star was bent with him. If bullets flew forward from here on, it would be she who took the brunt of their impact.

In the rear, ever gaining upon the fugitives, rode Suarez and his ragged banditos. Furious at this man who had sneaked into his own hidden camp and snatched the prize right from under his very nose, *El Jefe* was out for blood. Nothing would do but that the woman be recaptured and the man shot dead.

"There!"

Star raised her head. Something visible, far away. Some sort of wooden structure, out here in the wilds. "Refuge, Matt? Someone's house?"

"Not a house. Line shack, maybe. We can fight 'em off from there, Star. Y' know how t' fire a gun?"

Her expression was grim but determined. "Do I!"

He turned his head, long enough to send her a flash of the old confident grin. "Then we'll give 'em hell, girl. C'mon, stick with me."

"Always," she whispered, so low that the word was almost inaudible. Almost.

Some sort of shack it was, indeed, they discovered, clattering and crashing up to its very door. Not necessarily line, and not necessarily even habitable. Half small building, half stable, half some other edifice of no discernible purpose. For theirs, for now, it would do.

Paused outside, Star hastily slid to the ground, with Matt in similar haste throwing one leg over the horse's rump and dismounting. Then inside, Colonel and all, with the door slammed shut and a bar flung across.

Both stopped, breathing hard, to exchange disbelieving glances before taking stock of what lay around them, this empty and abandoned place.

"Not much t' look at," observed Matt grudgingly.

Large enough, certainly, with plenty of room to move throughout, even filled though it was by the stallion's very solid presence. Colonel's expression seemed as grudging as his owner's voice.

Several windows, half-covered by heavy wooden shutters. Walls whose planks fit together unevenly and awkwardly and, in some places, not at all. Walls, thought the Ranger, that could have used more substance when there was about to be a gun battle going on outside them. A stack of moldy straw in one corner, a couple of twig chairs, a roof through which glimpses of what promised to be a glorious sunset could be seen.

"Been a helluva day," was Matt's mild comment.

Star wasn't about to argue with that. "Helluva day," she agreed, with a tentative smile.

He grinned back. "Sit down for a bit, Star. May as well get settled in. C'mon, Colonel, hike yourself over and give us some space."

After the whirlwind events of the past hour or so, it was a relief to take a seat in one of the wobbly chairs, lean back, and simply let emotion wash away and exhaustion take over. She had hardly had time to think, since her handover from Franklin Bower to Suarez and his band of cutthroats. She had only reacted. And that from a position of panic, rather than strength.

While she engaged in some quiet time, highlighted by a golden ray of the dying sun, Matt took care of immediate chores. That meant he needed to uncinch and unsaddle the restive horse, remove the bit, and work over the lathered muscles with a currycomb.

"Here, Star," he broke softly into her meditations. "Your turn."

She opened her eyes, questioning, and looked up. Only to find him kneeling before her on the packed-earth floor, heavy brows furrowed and dark gaze intent.

"Yeah. That gang'll prob'ly be here any minute, and we need t' be ready for 'em. So let me look you over."

Both his saddlebag and war bag lay open beside him, with supplies out for use. Wetting the scarf sparingly with cool water from his canteen, he gently sponged her face and applied dabs of ointment to several of the more severe cuts. Injuries aplenty, but apparently superficial; none that would cause permanent scarring or flaws.

"Worked you over pretty good," he said, doing his best to remain impartial.

"Nothing," she returned quietly, "compared to what—to what—could have—"

"I'll see 'em all in jail for that. Or dead. All right, let's move on."

The ropes binding her had been tied tightly, and she had fought. The proof of that showed in the raw bloody marks encircling both wrists, angry as a chunk of fresh-cut beef. More ointment, this time patted onto the strips of soft old cotton he wrapped as bandages.

"Any place else?"

She shook her head. "No, that's about the worst. Thank you, Matt. I must look—quite a sight."

He had risen to stand nearby, surveying her with an unreadable expression. Long hair black and shiny as obsidian, bosom half-bared right down to a beribboned camisole by damage done, brave and beautiful and regal still despite all the wear and tear of her night to day ordeal.

"Oh, yeah, Miss Mendoza. You are that, all right—quite a sight."

An apricot flush crept over the high cheekbones, and unconsciously she tried to shrink down into her ruined shirtwaist.

"Oh. Sorry. Damn, Star, I always seem t' be apologizin' to you. Here, this should help."

Matt reached once more into the saddlebag for the spare shirt he always carried and held it out for her. Gratefully she slipped into the long sleeves, for cover and for warmth, and fastened the buttons firmly together over all that had drawn his attention and obvious admiration.

"Hey, you—inside! I wanna talk with you!"

He sent her a significant glance. "Company, Star." Revolver held cocked and ready, Matt moved to the front window, slightly shifted the shutter, and called out, "Don't wanna talk t' you, Suarez, unless it's through the bars of a jail cell. Take a powder."

"Hey, gringo! You got the girl, right?"

"What business is it of yours who I got? Get lost."

Talk, so the phrase goes, is cheap. While that cheap talk was going on, Matt was keeping a close eye on movement outside. Tall grass rustled, some thirty yards away, stood silent and still, rustled again. Only then did a bullet zing in to smack into the wood above his head. Instantly he returned fire. One, twice, again and again.

Shots rang out from the perimeter, in several directions. One of Matt's targets let out a howl and crashed onto the ground. More shots, from the back of the rickety building. Colonel, distinctly and decidedly uneasy, thumped around and whickered a little. Damned if *he* wanted to be served up as a bulls'-eye!

Another one down, bleeding profusely right out in the open.

In the pause to reload his Colt, he heard Suarez yell out one more challenge. "Hey, you gringo! I want that little *puta*! How about you hand her over to me, and maybe I let you live, eh?"

"*Besa mi culo, bastardo*!"

Star gasped.

"Oh, hell," mumbled Matt, shamefaced. "I forgot you speak Spanish. Sorry if I shocked your sensibilities."

A half-smile, more of tenderness than of amusement. "My sensibilities will have to go much farther than that to be shocked, Matthew Yancey. I was surprised, that's all."

Ziiiiiinnnng, splat! Like the sting of a nasty-tempered hornet, another bullet hurtled in. Then several, all at once.

Matt peered cautiously past the edge of the shutter. Nothing. The field was empty of banditos; even their horses were out of sight. Where had they disappeared to?

Suddenly another barrage hit the structure, like deadly hailstones. Matt fired valiantly away, hoping all the while that their refuge wouldn't fall apart.

More gunfire, but this time from inside. And not his. Startled, he turned for a quick look, only to discover Star at the opposite window, making good and efficient use of his Henry rifle. As evidenced by the scream of another outlaw, hit and apparently in a bad way.

Damn. Matt couldn't help grinning. This was some woman.

Three down and out of commission. How many left? Eight? Ten? Only half a dozen? Whatever the number, Suarez, witnessing the strength of their firepower, seemingly decided on a temporary reprieve. The bullets stopped, the shouting stopped. *Los banditos* had pulled back.

After a few minutes of absolute silence, during which not even the grasshoppers in the field dared make a sound, Star leaned against the wall she had been defending so valiantly and slid slowly to the ground. "Do you think they've gone?" she whispered.

Matt was still scrutinizing the area outside, shifting his scan from side to side. "Couldn't be so lucky. They're reconnoiterin'. Tryin' to wait us out. Later on, when it's full dark, and we're not seein' so well, and both of us are too tired t' think, I'm guessin' they'll try again."

The horse stamped a hoof, shifted position, rolled his eyes in his master's direction. *Are we about finished with all this?* His expression clearly asked. *I'm ready to hit the road.*

"Oh, Matt, I'm so sorry," she said sadly.

"Sorry?" Dumbfounded, he stared across the small space at her in the waning light. "What for?"

"For getting you mixed up in all this. For putting your life at risk. If not for my falling into Bower's trap, you wouldn't have come to my rescue, and you wouldn't be in this danger right now."

"Star. Sweet jumpin' Jesus." He scooted over, concerned that she might break down—might *really* break down—and who could blame her? After all this, most women would have been throwing a royal hissy fit of hysterics about now. Settled in beside her, nice and snug, Matt wrapped his strong left arm carefully around her shoulders and pulled her even closer. "We haven't had a chance yet t' talk things through. Like I said, it's been a helluva day. Let me tell you how mine started."

So there, during the lull between the last battle and whenever the next one would start, Matthew described his visit with Frances, upon her insistence, to Star's family home.

"You saw my mother?" repeated Star, wonderingly.

"Sure did. Adsila. Pretty name. What's it mean?"

"Blossom," said she, with a half-smile of remembrance. "Her name means blossom."

"Ahuh. Pretty name for a pretty woman. Anyway, as desperate as we were to see her, and find out what had happened t' you, she was just as desperate herself t' find somebody to give help. Seems your paw's brother…well, he's parta this gang shootin' up our shelter, here."

"Ricardo. But my father never speaks of him, he's the—well, I suppose you would say he's the black sheep of our family."

Matt nodded and squeezed her a little more tightly. She felt good, soft and warm in all the places a girl should feel soft and warm, and he liked the way she fit so well into the crook of his arm, next to his heart. "Black sheep or not, he done you a good turn, Star," Matt told her soberly. "He let your maw know what had happened t' you."

The story continued, from the conversation with Adsila that provided all the background details she had so long tried to hide, to the frantic race back to San Francisco, to the wild gallop all the way south along Glen Creek Road, using Ricardo's accurate directions to the camp.

"And there you were, by God," finished up Matt on a note of satisfaction. "Damn. I about passed out, just havin' that load off my mind, when I saw you back amongst the rocks."

"You can imagine my own reaction," said Star dryly.

A flash of the old familiar grin. "Think I can, at that. Don't think either of us ever wanna go through it again, either. Now, talk t' me. Tell me what happened that got you caught up in this mess."

"Oh, Matt." She sighed.

Despite their rough, cramped surroundings and the danger waiting somewhere outside, it was pure luxury to sit here beside him, snuggled close, sharing his thoughts and capturing his attention. If she died today, she wanted to die like this, in this man's company, in this man's care. He had come to mean too much to her, in too short a time, and she wished to never be out of his sight again.

His left hand was slowly caressing her upper arm, his left thigh lay against her, hard as wood and just about as sturdy. Matthew Yancey had today proven himself to be all that a Texas Ranger lays claim to be: loyal, honorable, dependable as dawn, ethical to a fault, and fiercely conscientious. How could she ever have doubted him and his motives?

"Is it that tough t' say?" he asked gently. His Colt had been laid aside, within reach, so that his right hand was free to lift her chin, forcing her eyes to meet his in the semi-dark. "Damn."

"What?"

"I wanna touch you, Star," he admitted. "But you're so bunged-up that I'm afraid I'll hurt you if I do."

"Not now," she agreed, the brilliance of her upward gaze reflecting her name. "But later—perhaps?"

"Later. Definitely. Think you can go on now?"

Most assuredly she could go on now. All outside still lay silent and ominous, giving no hint of what was to come. Before another confrontation, she must recount the happenings from yesterday morning until this desperate evening.

"I was taking my bath," she began.

As always ruthlessly honest with others as she was with herself, she spared nothing in the telling. That long night of disillusionment and woe, the tears, the conclusions reached—Star laid bare her heart, and under the bruised cheek she could feel a conscience-stricken wince of Matt's torso.

Then had come Bower's unexpected visit, his demands, his threats of blackmail.

"I was so worried about my mother, Matt," she diverged to admit. "If you talked with her, then you know—"

"I know. She told me all about her past, Star. And I think we can get that taken care of, so put any concerns about Adsila right outa your head for the moment."

Again that shining star-like regard of pure admiration. Seen thus, Matt felt suddenly ten feet tall and filled with miracles. He could lick his weight in catamounts, or climb a mountain barefoot, if necessary. What was a little Mexican outlaw gang to deal with, by comparison?

And so she'd surrendered to Franklin Bower. The ride to his ranch, the dress, the dinner, the attempted lovemaking…she told it all, every relentless word. At that last part, with Bower's obscene moves being made upon her, Matt let out a low animal growl, deep in his throat. Not as an interruption, but as an involuntary response. Let him but track down the filthy rancher, let him but return the favor of power reversed…!

"And then there's Raquel. She helped me, Matt. She helped me escape, but we were recaptured together, and I don't know what happened to her. We have to find her, and find her brother, too."

"We will, Star," he soothed, "we will. Just as soon as we can get outa this predicament."

"This—this bandito leader, this—Suarez—I was turned over to him, and to his men…early this morning. I don't know exactly when, Matt; sometime around dawn, when they arrived at the Condor. And they took me away…"

"Aw, Star." Matt, distressed by her distress, tightened his strong left arm around her, feeling her overwrought body weaken and shiver. "If I coulda been there—if I coulda stopped 'em—"

Her amber eyes darkened with remembered horror, with all that she had been forced to undergo during that ride south to the outlaw camp. "I was so—afraid, Matt. I didn't dare even hope that—that you might somehow…out of the blue…appear for me…"

"T' the gates of hell itself, Goldenstar Mendoza," he promised thickly.

"And when I looked up—and saw you there—" Tears had once again gathered, to pool and overflow. "I thought you were—a mirage, a dream…like when you're lost in the desert, and for thirst you begin to hallucinate…"

"Touch me, Star. Do I feel like a dream?"

Trembling, she lifted one hand to curve along his bearded cheek, in wonder and in gratitude. "No. You're solid. You're real. But you're still my dream. Matthew Yancey."

She let out a half-sob then that shook him to the marrow. Overcome, he suddenly pulled her quivering body up and over, to lie full-length atop his. Both big hands smoothed down over her arms in a slow caress, then moved flat along her spine, then cupped her backside with potency and power.

"My God, Star," he managed on a soft rumble, "I do love you so much, girl."

"Oh, Matt! I never thought—I never believed—"

"Believe, Star," he told her roughly. A very cautious, light kiss to her temple, as he adjusted her position upon what was becoming a most interested spectator to their drama, something that had stirred up to peer around with speculation and need. "When we get outa this—"

"You have plans?"

"Damn straight I have plans. Thought of nothin' else when I came barrelin' after you. Scared t' death I'd be too late. Scared t' death I might never find you at all." He enveloped her in a hug that came near to crushing her bones. "So, whaddya say, Star?"

Crushed bones or not, she was studying him with tenderness and devotion. "To what, Matthew?"

"Uh—you…me…if you feel the same way, that is."

"Matt. My rescuer. My Ranger. My man. How could I feel any other way? I love you, Matthew Yancey, with every breath of my lungs, with every pulse of my blood, with every throb of my heart." Suddenly, shockingly, helplessly, she giggled. "And, I think…with every yin force of my body, ready for the yang force of yours."

In a bold move that he never would have expected from this ladylike flower of womanhood, she slipped one palm between them, over his chest, his belly, his loin, and lower, to press and grasp all that awaited.

Matt gulped. "Sweet Jesus, Star," he let out a groan. "Doncha go—'

Bang; zzzzzzt; smack! One bullet sliced through the air to crack over their heads, joined by a volley of other bullets. Rejoined to the battle he had tried to forget, Matt thrust Star aside, grabbed his revolver, and took up position at the window. Accordingly, she reached for the rifle and took up position at the opposite wall. They had just a single instant to exchange one swift glance of love and mutual desire before hell started popping.

Full dark, but for the faint white gleam of a full moon overhead, had encompassed the meadow. Flashes of gunfire here and there lit up outlaw positions scattered through the grass, upon which the little structure's defenders could take aim and respond in kind. Behind them, Colonel, who had been happily dozing in his corner, woke at the noise and danced sideways with apprehension.

"We have come back, you yellow-spined gringo!" The taunts of Suarez burbled along, gloating and purposeful. "Is my little hostage still alive? I gave you time to think…and do. Have you used her yet as I mean to use her?"

For answer, Matt fired carefully and coolly at the disembodied voice. Every Ranger in his group could testify as to the accuracy of his shots. What he targeted, he hit.

Disembodied no more. Several smacks of a bullet plowing into vulnerable human flesh, a couple of yowls of pain, then silence. Over his shoulder, Matt gave a thumbs'-up sign to his companion.

Except that now the outlaws, apparently infuriated by the wounding—or killing—of their leader, had decided to set in with a vengeance. So much lead poured into the cabin, so many rounds and shells, that both Matt and Star dropped down, crawled to meet in a frantic embrace, and ducked for cover.

"Reckon we've riled up a hornet's nest?" he said in her ear.

"Maybe they will give up and go away again?" she wondered hopefully.

More gunfire, another horrendous deafening barrage. Oddly enough, however, the noise seemed to be approaching from another direction. From the north. Accompanied by yells, shouted curses, and the whinnies and neighs of excited horses.

"Star!" Matt raised himself off the dusty ground to kneel beside her, both hands curved around her skull in protective mode. He was grinning like the village idiot. "I think the cavalry has arrived!"

"Cavalry? But—what—I don't understand…who—"

"Sheriff William Goddard and his merry band of recruits, that's who!"

Outside, an occasional shot still rang across the meadow, but the hullabaloo was slowly dying down. Matt wasn't about to investigate yet; they would wait things out inside, in relative safety, until given the all-clear.

That came soon enough.

"Hello the house!" rumbled William. "Hold your fire, Matt. I'm comin' in!"

Surging upright, Matt unbarred and flung open the door. "Will, you ole bull moose. Never been so glad t' see anybody in my life! Well—" he glanced sideways at Star, who had risen and was brushing off her skirts, to amend, "except for this woman here."

Reaching out one long arm, he gathered her in to hold close and secure.

The sheriff carefully set his lighted lantern onto the least wobbly of the two chairs to look both rescuer and hostage up and down. Relief had brightened his features into great cheer. "Not much gladder than I am, Mr. Ranger man. You okay in here?"

Matt grinned. "Better'n okay. What's goin' on out there?"

"Oh, y' know, the usual. Catch a few outlaws, knock 'em around, tie 'em up. All in a day's work. Brought me a passel of deputies, after settlin' the plague problem down by the docks, and they're takin' care of things as we speak."

"Ahuh. D'ja find Suarez in that mess?"

"The leader? Hell, yes. Bleedin' like a stuck pig and yellin' for some help, when we come upon him. You wanna run on out and say howdy-do? Maybe give him a big sloppy kiss?"

"Yeah, I'd like t' give him somethin', all right."

Man talk briefly and temporarily put aside, William turned his attention to the center of this dramatic turmoil. "You doin' all right, Star?" Even in the fragile lamplight he could see how badly she had been treated, and the dark lines of exhaustion and horror beneath her eyes.

"You may not think it to look at me, Will," she answered, smiling like a Madonna, "but I am doing just wonderfully."

"Ah. That's good, then." The last thing he needed to deal with on this busy night was a female's histrionics, justified or not.

Subdued sounds from whatever was taking place outside— shouts, and the cringe worthy noise of fists slammed into flesh, and heated words in Spanish and English—reached them. Back to reality.

"So, you wanna hear some o' this now, my friend, or as we head back north?"

Matt chuckled. "Definitely now, Will. Not one of your long-winded stories, though. I'm lookin' to get this girl home before she collapses on me."

"Huh. Well, then."

Suarez had led his crew of banditos like a typical bully, with intimidation and threats. Now, caught, handcuffed, about to face prison, he was singing like a sweet wood thrush.

"Man, he's confessin' to crimes I never knew he was involved in," Will said in awe, shaking his head. "Should be a great day when they land him in court. Anyway, Star, he killed Franklin Bower."

"What?" From being tucked wearily into the comforting crook of Matt's shoulder she jerked upright, astounded. "He's dead? Truly?"

"Truly. Suarez just told us so, outside. Guess that'll mean a trip to the Condor. Seems the outlaw was gettin' impatient with some of what Bower had done, and after he took you he planned on no more business between the two of 'em any more. Rustlin', Matt, and murder, and drugs. So that meant gettin' rid of his main man to head south permanently."

Star tugged at Matt's sleeve. "Raquel. Then we can go along with everyone, and find her, and release all those men at the silver mine."

"Raquel? Silver mine?" Sheriff Will's jaw dropped. "Y' mean there's still more goin' on?"

"Oh, Will," said Matt. His voice rang almost with pity for the lawman and the mountains of paperwork that would be involved, once this investigation had been completed and all the details worked out. "You sorry son-of-a-bitch. So much t' look forward to!"

"Huh. Then we'd better get crackin'." Will took a minute to plan arrangements for what must be done next. "We got us two dead outlaws out there, three wounded, and six still up and kickin'. I'll send half my troops back to the city with the prisoners. The other half can come along with us, off to the Condor." In the dim light his kindly eyes ranged over the wavering figure of Matt's charge. "You sure you wanna come with, Star? You gonna hold up okay?"

She looked up at the man beside her, wearing such a beatific expression of love and adoration as to blur the eyesight and stutter the heartbeat. "Absolutely, I will hold up. We need to do this. We need to finish what Bower started. May I ride with you, Matt?"

Not so strange that he, mere mortal, was wearing the same expression. "Absolutely. In front, this time, where I can keep good hold on you." *And whatever parts he could easily reach.*

Chapter 10

"The month of September is beautiful for a wedding," sniffled Sarah, from her pew in the First Mission Church.

"So's October," twinkled William, from her left. His right hand snaked up from the wooden seat to rest proprietarily on her thigh. "But then you must be aware, Sarah, girl, since that's the month you decided on. And more shame t' you, keepin' me on tenterhooks that much longer."

She flashed him a pert glance. With her double dimples much in evidence, the effect was stunning, and her betrothed reeled under it. "No more so than you keeping me on tenterhooks for a long time yourself, Will Goddard."

He rumbled with subdued laughter. "Wasn't planned that way, sweetheart. If you recall, me and my whole office and Matthew himself got pretty bogged down there for a while. Couldn't exactly take care of my own personal plans with everythin' else goin' on."

Everything else going on, indeed. And what a crowded few weeks it had been!

With the *Los Huesos Banditos* gang broken up and carted away by half the law force to the welcoming depths of San Francisco's largest hoosegow, William had led the rest of his men, along with Matt and Star, homeward, veering off only toward the Condor Ranch. There, they found the situation chaotic.

Just that very morning, Horace, Franklin Bower's less-than-adoring manservant, had discovered the quite bullet-riddled, quite lifeless body of his erstwhile employer sprawled face-down in the dust. Shocked, and yet not so shocked—having a very good idea of all the nefarious activity in which Bower had been involved—Horace had dispatched one of the *vaqueros* for the local undertaker. And a coffin.

Then he had set about packing his own essentials. By hook or by crook, he was definitely leaving for London on the first ship out of San Francisco harbor. It was way past time to shake the dirt of this miserable state from his polished boots and seek out his English Lord, in hopes of a truce.

"And Raquel?" Star demanded anxiously from the warmth of Matt's encircling, supportive arms. "Where is she, have you seen her?"

"Indeed I have, Miss." Horace had surveyed her, brow cocked with surprise. How circumstances do change, and how the mighty do sometimes fall! "Mr. Bower ordered me to lock her in the storeroom for a—I believe he termed it a 'cooling-off period.' And there she has stayed."

"In the storeroom!" Furious, Star had thrust herself to the ground and away, pelting into the house with a flurry of filthy, travel-worn skirts. Which left Matt no choice but to follow.

Another rescue of a battered, beaten girl. Too bad Bower was dead, thought Matt dispassionately, as he watched the two hugging and weeping. He would have taken pure delight in doing some battering and beating on the rancher himself.

At that juncture, hearing more details about the ongoing horrific enslavement at the silver mine, Will had decided it would be necessary for the group to return home for rest, rations, and reinforcements before tackling the next problem on his agenda.

"B'sides," he had noted, "both these little gals are fagged out. Best get 'em off to bed somewheres they can sleep."

Matt wouldn't have dreamed of arguing with that salient point. Now, if it could only have been *his* bed…

Leaving general instructions for the ranch staff to proceed as usual until arrangements could be made, sending Raquel to pack up her belongings, William had commandeered a wagon from the

Condor's stable, along with a couple of horses. The whole troop had set off for the city with a general air of relief and a sense of light-heartedness for what had been accomplished thus far.

Returning Star to her cabin, with Raquel as an unexpected guest who soon gratefully collapsed in the bedroom, Matt had been disposed to linger. After all that had happened, he wanted only to stay, to bill and coo with his lady love. And who could blame him? Especially with such a willing—no, eager—participant.

But eventually fatigue overcame them both. Short of spending the rest of the night there, Matt was forced to take his leave, in such a state of arousal that only a long, cool before-dawn walk gave him respite.

And then it was on to his own home, to greet his excited, enthusiastic son next morning and offer information and an explanation to his worried housekeeper. One more task awaited him: making sure Frances paid another visit to Adsila Mendoza, to bring her up-to-date about current developments and provide reassurance as to her daughter's safety.

Next day's trip, locked and loaded and armed for bear, a force much increased in numbers had departed for the east, heading into the area containing Bower's silver mine as described by Raquel, from details in her brother's letter.

"Dunno how long we'll be gone," Matt had said quietly, on the threshold early that morning. One boot in, one boot out; longing to remain, needing to depart. "It's a far piece, and slow goin' across the state, with a wagon, a bunch of peace officers, and lawmen from every agency Will could think of."

"And where is this?"

"Toward the Sierra Nevadas," he explained, "near some place called Juliet Camp. And God knows what we'll find when we get there."

Star's eyes searched his beloved features. "Dangerous, Matt?"

"Dunno that either, Star, girl."

Meaningless to add words of caution, or discretion. He would be as careful as he could be. That was it.

With a little shiver of foreboding, she stepped into his open arms, hiding her bruised face against his pine-scented shirtfront. "Come back to me, Matthew Yancey," she whispered. "Promise that you will come back to me. Swear it."

His big hand smoothed down over the thick black hair, done up now in a heavy knot. "Why, Star, sweetheart, o' course I'm comin' back to you." Head bowed, she did not see but sensed his lopsided smile. "We got us a weddin' t' plan for."

For ten days the posse—for so it was, consisting of constabulary that increased as it rolled along, like a snowball gathering force and speed—engaged in their crime-fighting venture,while those staying behind counted the hours until their safe return.

And then suddenly they were home again, every one of them, to report a rousing success. The slave labor had been freed, guards taken into custody, families reunited—chiefly Benito and his overjoyed sister, Raquel. Even the governor had gotten involved. No accidents or deaths, but several wounded. One of whom was Matt.

"I promised I'd come back," he said a trifle crossly from his seat of honor on Star's settee, protesting the fuss made by his son, his housekeeper, and, most of all, his sweetheart. "I didn't say I'd come back whole."

"You hush now," Star ordered with touching severity. "Just sit there, and don't move or I will put opiates in your tea to make you sleep. And you know I can do it, too. A bullet through the arm is nothing to make light of, Mr. Yancey. I am here to take care of you. I will serve your every need. I will—"

"*Every* need?" Matt cocked his head to one side, eyes glinting with mischief. "Well, let me tell you, I've got some needs, all right. C'mere, Star."

Now Matt, fully recovered, stood nervously waiting near the front of the church for his bride. His five-year-old son stood happily waiting beside him. His good friend Frances stood proudly waiting across from him. His future mother-in-law sat uncertainly yet hopefully waiting in the front pew.

For all her invaluable help in tracking down the *Los Huesos* bunch, Adsila Mendoza had been granted a full pardon by the governor and could walk anywhere freely and by safe passage. Her husband, Daniel, a handsome mustachioed man who would shortly be escorting his daughter down the aisle, couldn't stop beaming about the many boons being suddenly granted during these past few tumultuous weeks.

All of Matt's brothers were present. Eight of them had thrown aside business matters and personal affairs to attend, without regard to cost. Even though the Civil War was still raging across the continent, they had somehow managed to find transportation in order to attend. The ninth, John, who had recently returned from Boston with his new wife, Cecelia, was parked near the front for support.

"Her wedding gown is gorgeous," murmured Cecelia, as Star drifted by in a simple, cool dress of ivory lace satin and tulle. "And so is she."

"Huh, sure is," whispered her husband in return. "But I got me the cream of the crop."

Despite an understandable case of nerves, Star was able to glance around as she proceeded on her father's arm toward the altar, where flickering candles beckoned and the good pastor stood ready. Daniel smiled down at her. The small crowd of guests smiled up at her. Her groom smiled across at her.

And then he winked.

THE END

Book Links

<u>Books 1-10 in Taking the High Road Series</u>

Book 1: John Yancey (Free book)
https://www.amazon.com/dp/B00QH2FD98

Book 2: Matthew Yancey
https://www.amazon.com/dp/B00RAT7DYK

Book 3: James Yancey
https://www.amazon.com/dp/B00S3YP280

Book 4: Thomas Yancey
https://www.amazon.com/dp/B00T727PKK

Book 5: Travis Yancey
https://www.amazon.com/dp/B00U1DALKU

Book 6: Nathaniel Yancey
https://www.amazon.com/dp/B00UZOWEIW

Book 7: Benton Yancey
https://www.amazon.com/dp/B00W1S9AWS

Book 8: Paul Yancey
https://www.amazon.com/dp/B00X75EYUM

Book 9: Cole Yancey
https://www.amazon.com/dp/B00ZG8CI6K

Book 10: Rob Yancey
https://www.amazon.com/dp/B01382OVEM

Thank You

Dear Reader,

Thank you for choosing to read my books out of the thousands that merit reading. I recognize that reading takes time and quietness, so I am grateful that you have designed your lives to allow for this enriching endeavor, whatever the book's title and subject.

Now more than ever before, Amazon reviews and Social Media play vital role in helping individuals make their reading choices. If any of my books have moved you, inspired you, or educated you, please share your reactions with others by posting an Amazon review as well as via email, Facebook, Twitter, Goodreads, -- or even old-fashioned face-to-face conversation! And when you receive my announcement of my new book, please pass it along. Thank you.

For updates about New Releases, as well as exclusive promotions, visit my website and sign up for the VIP mailing list. Click here to get started: www.morrisfenrisbooks.com

I invite you to connect with me through Social media:

1. Facebook :
   https://www.facebook.com/AuthorMorrisFenris/
2. Twitter: https://twitter.com/morris_fenris
3. Pinterest: https://www.pinterest.com/AuthorMorris/
4. Instagram:
   https://www.instagram.com/authormorrisfenris/

For my portfolio of books on Amazon, please visit my Author Page:

Amazon USA:
amazon.com/author/morrisfenris

Amazon UK:
https://www.amazon.co.uk/Morris%20Fenris/e/B00FXLWKRC

You can also contact me by email:
authormorrisfenris@gmail.com

With profound gratitude, and with hope for your continued reading pleasure,

Morris Fenris
Author & Publisher

Made in United States
Orlando, FL
01 November 2021

10157599R00065